SELECTED GRIMM FAIRY TALES

The Brothers Grimm

Legend Press Ltd, 51 Gower Street, London, WC1E 6HJ
info@legendpress.co.uk | www.legendpress.co.uk

Print ISBN 978-1-78955-9-484
Ebook ISBN 978-1-78955-9-491
Set in Times. Printing managed by Jellyfish Solutions Ltd.
Cover design by Anna Morrison | www.annamorrison.com

Once upon a time, there was a brother named **Jacob** and another named **Wilhelm**, and they were among the first and best-known collectors of German and European folk tales. By the end of their life, they had become responsible for immortalising our most iconic stories: Cinderella, Hansel and Gretel, Rapunzel, Sleeping Beauty, Snow White, and more. Their collections have endured since the 1800s, and are now available in more than 100 languages.

Contents

LITTLE BRIAR-ROSE

A long time ago, there were a King and Queen who said every day, "Ah, if only we had a child!" but they never had one.

But it happened that once when the Queen was bathing, a Frog crept out of the water on to the land, and said to her, "Your wish shall be fulfilled. Before a year has gone by, you shall have a daughter."

What the Frog had said came true, and the Queen had a little girl, who was so pretty that the King could not contain himself for joy, and ordered a great feast. He invited not only his kindred, friends and acquaintance, but also the Wise Women, in order that they might be kind and well-disposed toward the child. There were thirteen of them in his kingdom. But, as he had only twelve golden plates for them to eat out of, one of them had to be left at home.

The feast was held with all manner of splendor. When it came to an end the Wise Women bestowed their magic gifts upon the baby. One gave Virtue, another Beauty, a third Riches, and so on with everything in the world that one can wish for.

When eleven of them had made their promises, suddenly the thirteenth came in. She wished to avenge herself for not having been invited, and without greeting, or even looking at any one, she cried with a loud voice, "The King's Daughter, in her fifteenth year, shall prick herself with a spindle, and fall down dead." And, without saying a word more, she turned round and left the room.

They were all shocked. But the twelfth, whose good wish still remained unspoken, came forward, and as she could not undo the evil sentence, but only soften it, she said, "It shall not be death, but a deep sleep of a hundred years, into which the Princess shall fall."

The King, who wished to keep his dear child from the misfortune, gave orders that every spindle in the whole kingdom should be burnt. Meanwhile, the gifts of the Wise Women were fulfilled on the young girl, for she was so beautiful, modest, sweet tempered, and wise, that every one who saw her, was bound to love her.

It happened that on the very day, when she was fifteen years old, the King and Queen were not at home, and the maiden was left in the palace quite alone. So she went round into all sorts of places, looked into rooms and bedchambers just as she liked, and at last came to an old tower. She climbed up the narrow winding-staircase, and reached a little door. A rusty key was in the lock, and when she turned it the door sprang open. There in a little room sat an Old Woman with a spindle, busily spinning flax.

"Good day, old Dame," said the King's Daughter; "what are you doing there?"

"I am spinning," said the Old Woman, and nodded her head.

"What sort of thing is that, which rattles round so merrily?" said the maiden, and she took the spindle and wanted to spin too. But scarcely had she touched the spindle when the magic decree was fulfilled, and she pricked her finger with it.

And, in the very moment when she felt the prick, she fell down upon the bed that stood there, and lay in a deep sleep. And this sleep extended over the whole palace.

The King and Queen, who had just come home, and had entered the great hall, began to go to sleep, and the whole of the Court with them. The horses, too, went to sleep in the stable, the dogs in the yard, the pigeons upon the roof, the flies on the wall. Even the fire, that was flaming on the hearth, became quiet and slept. The roast meat left off frizzling, and the cook, who was just going to pull the hair of the scullery boy, because he had forgotten something, let him go, and went to sleep. And the wind fell; and on the trees before the castle not a leaf moved again.

But round about the castle, there began to grow a hedge of thorns. Every year it became higher, and at last grew close up round the castle and all over it, so that there was nothing of it to be seen, not even the flag upon the roof.

But the story of the beautiful sleeping "Briar-Rose," for so the Princess was named, went about the country, so that from time to time Kings' Sons came and tried to get through the thorny hedge into the castle. But they found it impossible, for the thorns held fast together, as if they had hands, and the youths were caught in them, could not get loose again, and died a miserable death.

After long, long years, again a King's Son came to that country. He heard an old man talking about the thorn-hedge, and that a castle was said to stand behind it in which a wonderfully beautiful Princess, named Briar-Rose, had been asleep for a hundred years; and that the King and Queen and the whole Court were asleep likewise. He had heard, too, from his grandfather, that many Kings' Sons had come, and had tried to get through the thorny hedge, but they had remained sticking fast in it, so had died a pitiful death.

Then the youth said, "I am not afraid. I will go and see the beautiful Briar-Rose." The good old man might dissuade him as he would, he did not listen to his words.

But by this time the hundred years had just passed. The day was come when Briar-Rose was to awake again. When the King's Son came near to the thorn-hedge, it was nothing but large and beautiful flowers, which parted from each other of their own accord, and let him pass unhurt. Then they closed again behind him like a hedge.

In the castle yard he saw the horses and the spotted hounds lying asleep. On the roof, sat the pigeons with their heads under their wings. And when he entered the house, the flies were asleep upon the wall, the cook in the kitchen was still holding out his hand to seize the boy, and the maid was sitting by the black hen which she was going to pluck.

He went on farther, and in the great hall he saw the whole of the Court lying asleep, and by the throne lay the King and Queen.

Then he went on still farther, and all was so quiet that a breath could be heard. At last he came to the tower, and opened the door into the little room where Briar-Rose was sleeping. There she lay, so beautiful that he could not turn his eyes away. He stooped down and gave her a kiss. But as soon as he kissed her, Briar-Rose opened her eyes and awoke, and looked at him quite sweetly.

Then they went down together, and the King awoke, and the Queen, and the whole Court, and gazed at each other in great astonishment. And the horses in the courtyard stood up and shook themselves. The hounds jumped up and wagged their tails. The pigeons upon the roof pulled out their heads from under their wings, looked round, and flew into the open country. The flies on the wall crept again. The fire in the kitchen burned up and flickered and cooked the meat. The joint began to turn and frizzle, and the cook gave the boy such a box on the ear that he screamed, and the maid plucked the fowl ready for the spit.

And then the marriage of the King's Son and Briar-Rose was celebrated with all splendor, and they lived contented to the end of their days.

THE SIX SWANS

Once upon a time, a certain King was hunting in a great forest, and he chased a wild beast so eagerly that none of his attendants could follow him. When evening drew near, he stopped and looked around him, and saw that he had lost his way. He sought a way out, but could find none. Then he perceived an Old Woman with a head which nodded all the time, who came toward him, but she was a Witch.

"Good woman," said he to her, "can you not show me the way through the forest?"

"Oh, yes, Lord King," she answered, "that I certainly can, but on one condition, and if you do not fulfill that, you will never get out of the forest, and will die of hunger in it."

"What kind of a condition is it?" asked the King.

"I have a daughter," said the old woman, "who is as beautiful as any one in the world, and well deserves to be your wife. If you will make her your Queen, I will show you the way out of the forest."

In the anguish of his heart the King consented, and the old woman led him to her little hut, where her daughter was sitting by the fire. She received the King as if she had been expecting him. He saw that she was very beautiful, but still she did not please him, and he could not look at her without secret horror.

After he had taken the maiden up on his horse, the old woman showed him the way, and the King reached his royal palace again, where the wedding was celebrated.

The King had already been married once, and had by his first wife, seven children, six boys and a girl, whom he loved better than anything else in the world. As he now feared that the new Queen might not treat them well, and even do them some injury, he took them to a lonely castle which stood in the midst of a forest. It lay concealed, and the way was so difficult to find, that he himself would not have found it at all, if a Wise Woman had not given him a ball of yarn with wonderful properties. When he threw it down before him, it unrolled itself and showed him his path.

The King, however, went so frequently to visit his dear children, that the Queen noticed his absence. She was curious and wanted to know what he did when he was alone in the forest. She gave a great deal of money to his servants, and they betrayed the secret to her, and told her likewise of the ball which alone could point out the way.

And now she knew no rest until she had learnt where the King kept the ball of yarn. Then she made little shirts of white silk, and as she had learnt the art of witchcraft from her mother, she sewed a charm inside them. And one day, when the King had ridden forth to hunt, she took the little shirts and went into the forest, and the ball showed her the way.

The children, who saw from a distance that some one was approaching, thought that their dear father was coming to them, and full of joy, ran to meet him. Then she threw one of the little shirts over each of them. And no sooner had the shirts touched their bodies than they were changed into Swans, and flew away over the forest.

The Queen went home quite delighted, and thought she had got rid of all the children, but the girl had not run out with her brothers, and the Queen knew nothing about her.

Next day, the King went to visit his children, but found no one but the little girl.

"Where are your brothers?" asked the King.

"Alas, dear Father," she answered, "they have gone away and left me alone!" and she told him that she had seen from her little window, how her brothers had flown away over the forest in the shape of Swans. And she showed him the feathers, which they had let fall in the courtyard, and which she had picked up.

The King mourned, but he did not think that the Queen had done this wicked deed. And as he feared that the girl also would be stolen from him, he wanted to take her away. But she was afraid of the Queen, and entreated the King to let her stay just one night more in the forest-castle.

The poor girl thought, "I can no longer remain here. I will go and seek my brothers." And when night came, she ran away, and went straight into the forest.

She walked the whole night long, and next day also without stopping, until she could go no farther for weariness. Then she saw a forest-hut, and went into it, and found a room with six little beds. She did not venture to get into any of them, but crept under one, and lay down on the hard ground, to pass the night there. Just before sunset she heard a rustling, and saw six Swans come flying in at the window. They alighted on the ground and blew at each other, and blew all the feathers off, and their swan's skins stripped off like a shirt.

Then the maiden looked at them and recognized her brothers. She rejoiced and crept forth from beneath the bed. The brothers were not less delighted to see their little sister, but their joy was short.

"Here can you not abide," they said to her. "This is a shelter for robbers. If they come home and find you, they will kill you."

"But can you not protect me?" asked the little sister.

"No," they replied, "only for one quarter of an hour each

evening, can we lay aside our swan's skins and have our human form. After that, we are once more turned into Swans."

The little sister wept, and said, "Can you not be set free?"

"Alas, no," they answered, "the conditions are too hard! For six years you may neither speak nor laugh, and in that time you must sew together six little shirts of Star-Flowers for us. And if one single word falls from your lips, all your work will be lost."

And when the brothers had said this, the quarter of an hour was over, and they flew out of the window again as Swans.

The maiden, however, resolved to deliver her brothers, even if it should cost her her life. She left the hut, went into the midst of the forest, seated herself on a tree, and there passed the night. Next morning, she went out and gathered Star-Flowers and began to sew. She could not speak to any one, and she had no wish to laugh. She sat there and looked at nothing but her work.

When she had spent a long time there, it came to pass that the King of the country was hunting in the forest, and his huntsmen came to the tree on which the maiden was sitting.

They called to her, and said, "Who are you?" But she made no answer. "Come down to us," said they. "We will not do you any harm."

She only shook her head. As they pressed her further with questions, she threw her golden necklace down to them, and thought to content them with that. They, however, did not cease, and then she threw her girdle down to them, and as this also was to no use, her garters, and little by little everything which she had on that she could do without, until she had nothing left but her shift. The huntsmen, however, did not let themselves be turned aside by that, but climbed the tree and fetched the maiden down and led her before the King.

The King asked, "Who are you? What are you doing on the tree?"

But she did not answer. He put the question in every language that he knew, but she remained as mute as a fish.

As she was so beautiful, the King's heart was touched, and he was smitten with a great love for her. He put his mantle on her, took her before him on his horse, and carried her to his castle.

Then he caused her to be dressed in rich garments, and she shone in her beauty like bright daylight, but no word could be drawn from her. He placed her by his side at table, and her modest bearing and courtesy pleased him so much, that he said, "She is the one whom I wish to marry, and no other woman in the world." And a few days after, he united himself to her.

The King, however, had a wicked mother, who was dissatisfied with his marriage and spoke ill of the young Queen. "Who knows," said she, "from whence comes the creature, who can't speak? She is not worthy of a King!"

After a year had passed, when the Queen brought her first child into the world, the old woman took it away from her and smeared her mouth with blood as she slept. Then she went to the King and accused the Queen of being a man-eater. The King would not believe it, and would not suffer any one to do her injury. She, however, sat continually sewing at the shirts, and cared for nothing else.

The next time, when she again bore a beautiful boy, the false old woman used the same treachery, but the King could not bring himself to believe her words. He said, "She is too pious and good to do anything of that kind. If she were not dumb, and could defend herself, her innocence would come to light."

But when the old woman stole away the newly-born child for the third time, and accused the Queen, who did not utter one word of defense, the King could do no otherwise than deliver her over to justice; and she was sentenced to be burned.

When the day came for the sentence to be executed, it was the last day of the six years during which she was not to speak or laugh, and she had delivered her dear brothers from the power of the enchantment. The six shirts were ready, only the left sleeve of the sixth was wanting.

When, therefore, she was led to the stake, she laid the shirts on her arm. And when she stood on high and the fire was just going to be lighted, she looked around and six Swans came flying through the air toward her. Then she saw that her deliverance was near, and her heart leapt with joy.

The Swans swept toward her and sank down so that she could throw the shirts over them. And as they were touched by them, their swan's skins fell off, and her brothers stood in their own form before her, vigorous and handsome. The youngest lacked only his left arm, and had in its place a swan's wing on his shoulder.

They embraced and kissed each other, and the Queen went to the King, who was greatly moved, and she began to speak, and said, "Dearest Husband, now I may speak and declare to you that I am innocent, and falsely accused." And she told him of the treachery of the old woman who had taken away her three children, and hidden them.

To the great joy of the King, they were brought back. And as a punishment, the wicked woman was bound to the stake and burned to ashes.

But the King and the Queen, with their six brothers, lived many years in happiness and peace.

RAPUNZEL

There was once a man and a woman, who had long in vain wished for a child. At length, the woman hoped that God was about to grant her desire.

These people had a little window at the back of their house from which a splendid garden could be seen. It was full of the most beautiful flowers and herbs. It was, however, surrounded by a high wall, and no one dared to go into it because it belonged to a Witch, who had great power and was dreaded by all the world.

One day, the woman was standing by this window and looking down into the garden, when she saw a bed which was planted with the most beautiful rampion (rapunzel), and it looked so fresh and green that she longed for it, and had the greatest desire to eat some.

This desire increased every day, and as she knew that she could not get any of it, she quite pined away, and looked pale and miserable.

Then her husband was alarmed, and asked, "What ails you, dear Wife?"

"Ah," she replied, "if I can't get some of the rampion to eat, which is in the garden behind our house, I shall die."

The man, who loved her, thought, "Sooner than let your wife die, bring her some of the rampion yourself, let it cost you what it will!"

In the twilight of evening, he clambered over the wall into the garden of the Witch, hastily clutched a handful of rampion, and took it to his wife. She at once made herself a salad of it, and ate it with much relish.

She, however, liked it so much – so very much – that the next day she longed for it three times as much as before. If he was to have any rest, her husband must once more descend into the garden. In the gloom of evening, therefore, he let himself down again. But when he had clambered down the wall he was terribly afraid, for he saw the Witch standing before him.

"How dare you," said she with angry look, "descend into my garden and steal my rampion like a thief? You shall suffer for it!"

"Ah," answered he, "let mercy take the place of justice! I had to do it out of necessity. My wife saw your rampion from the window, and felt such a longing for it that she would have died, if she had not got some to eat."

Then the Witch let her anger be softened, and said to him, "If the case be as you say, I will allow you to take away with you as much rampion as you will, only I make one condition, you must give me the child which your wife will bring into the world. It shall be well treated, and I will care for it like a mother."

The man in his terror consented to everything, and when the woman at last had a little daughter, the Witch appeared at once, gave the child the name of Rapunzel, and took it away with her.

Rapunzel grew into the most beautiful child beneath the sun. When she was twelve years old, the Witch shut her into a tower, which lay in a forest, and had neither stairs nor door. But quite at the top was a little window. When the Witch wanted to go in, she placed herself beneath this, and cried:

"Rapunzel, Rapunzel,
Let down thy hair."

Rapunzel had magnificent long hair, fine as spun gold, and when she heard the voice of the Witch, she unfastened her braided tresses and wound them round one of the hooks of the window above. And then the hair fell twenty ells down, and the Witch climbed up by it.

After a year or two, it came to pass that the King's Son rode through the forest and went by the tower. Then he heard a song, which was so charming that he stood still and listened. This was Rapunzel, who in her solitude passed her time in letting her sweet voice resound.

The King's Son wanted to climb up to her, and looked for the door of the tower, but none was to be found. He rode home, but the singing had so deeply touched his heart, that every day he went out into the forest and listened to it.

Once when he was thus standing behind a tree, he saw that a Witch came there, and he heard how she cried:

"Rapunzel, Rapunzel,
Let down thy hair."

Then Rapunzel let down the braids of her hair, and the Witch climbed up to her.

"If that is the ladder by which one mounts, I will for once try my fortune," said he.

The next day when it began to grow dark, he went to the tower and cried:

"Rapunzel, Rapunzel,
Let down thy hair."

Immediately the hair fell down, and the King's Son climbed up.

At first Rapunzel was terribly frightened when a man, such

as her eyes had never yet beheld, came to her. But the King's Son began to talk to her quite like a friend, and told her that his heart had been so stirred, that it had let him have no rest, so he had been forced to see her.

Then Rapunzel lost her fear, and when he asked her if she would take him for her husband, and she saw that he was young and handsome, she thought, "He will love me more than old Dame Gothel does;" and she said yes, and laid her hand in his.

She said also, "I will willingly go away with you, but I do not know how to get down. Bring with you a skein of silk every time that you come, and I will weave a ladder with it. When that is ready I will descend, and you will take me on your horse."

They agreed that until that time, he should come to her every evening, for the old woman came by day. The Witch remarked nothing of this, until once Rapunzel said to her, "Tell me, Dame Gothel, how it happens that you are so much heavier for me to draw up, than the young King's Son – he is with me in a moment."

"Ah! you wicked Child!" cried the Witch. "What do I hear you say! I thought I had separated you from all the world, and yet you have deceived me!"

In her anger she clutched Rapunzel's beautiful tresses, wrapped them twice round her left hand, seized a pair of scissors with the right, and *snip, snap,* they were cut off, and the lovely braids lay on the ground. And she was so pitiless that she took poor Rapunzel into a desert, where she had to live in great grief and misery.

On the same day, however, that she cast out Rapunzel, the Witch, in the evening, fastened the braids of hair which she had cut off, to the hook of the window; and when the King's Son came and cried:

> *"Rapunzel, Rapunzel,*
> *Let down thy hair,"*

she let the hair down.

The King's Son ascended. He did not find his dearest Rapunzel above, but the Witch, who gazed at him with wicked and venomous looks.

"Aha!" she cried mockingly, "you would fetch your dearest! But the beautiful bird sits no longer singing in the nest. The cat has got it, and will scratch out your eyes as well. Rapunzel is lost to you! You will never see her more!"

The King's Son was beside himself with grief and in his despair he leapt down from the tower. He escaped with his life, but the thorns into which he fell, pierced his eyes. Then he wandered quite blind about the forest, ate nothing but roots and berries, and did nothing but lament and weep over the loss of his dearest wife.

Thus he roamed about in misery for some years, and at length came to the desert where Rapunzel lived in wretchedness. He heard a voice, and it seemed so familiar to him that he went toward it. When he approached, Rapunzel knew him, and fell on his neck and wept. Two of her tears wetted his eyes and they grew clear again, and he could see with them as before.

He led her to his Kingdom where he was joyfully received, and they lived for a long time, happy and contented.

MOTHER HOLLE

There was once a widow who had two daughters, one of whom was beautiful and industrious, whilst the other was ugly and lazy. But she was much fonder of the ugly and lazy one. Every day, the other, poor girl, had to sit by a well in the highway, and *spin, spin* till her fingers bled.

Now it happened, one day, that the shuttle was stained with her blood. She dipped it in the well to wash the stains off, and it dropped out of her hand and fell to the bottom. She began to weep, and ran to the woman, and told her of the mishap.

She scolded her hard, and was so cruel as to say, "Since you have let the shuttle fall in, you must fetch it out again."

So the girl went back to the well, and did not know what to do. Then in the anguish of her heart, she jumped into the well to get the shuttle. She lost her senses. But when she awoke and came to herself, she was in a lovely meadow, where the sun was shining and thousands of flowers were growing.

Along this meadow she went, and at length came to a baker's oven full of bread. And the bread cried:

> *"Oh, take me out! Take me out!*
> *Or I shall burn. I am well baked!"*

So she went up to it, and, with the bread shovel, took out all the loaves one after the other.

After that, she went on till she came to a tree covered with apples, and it called to her:

> *"Oh, shake me! Shake me!*
> *We apples are all ripe!"*

So she shook the tree till the apples fell like rain, and went on shaking till they were all down. And when she had gathered them into a heap, she went on her way.

At last, she came to a little house out of which an Old Woman was peeping. She had such large teeth that the girl was frightened, and was about to run away.

But the Old Woman called out to her, "What are you afraid of, my Child? Stay with me. If you will do the work in my house carefully, you shall be the better for it! Only you must take care to make my bed well, and to shake it thoroughly till the feathers fly – for then it snows on earth. I am Mother Holle."

As the Old Woman spoke so kindly to her, the girl took heart, and willingly entered her service. She did everything to the Old Woman's satisfaction, and always shook her bed so hard that the feathers flew about like snowflakes. So she lived happily with her, never an angry word, and boiled or roasted meat every day.

She stayed some time with Mother Holle, then she grew sad. At first she did not know what was the matter with her, but, by and by, she found that it was homesickness. Although she was many thousand times better off here than at home, still she had a longing to be there.

At last, she said to the Old Woman, "I am longing for home. However well off I am down here, I cannot stay any longer. I must go up again to my own people."

Mother Holle said, "I am pleased that you long for your

home again. You have served me so faithfully, that I myself will take you up again."

Thereupon she took her by the hand, and led her to a large door. The door was opened, and just as the girl was standing beneath the doorway, a heavy shower of Gold-Rain fell, and all the gold stuck to her so that she was covered with it.

"You shall have that because you are so industrious," said Mother Holle. And at the same time, she gave her back the shuttle which she had let fall into the well.

Thereupon the door closed, and the girl found herself again upon the earth, not far from her mother's house.

As she went into the yard, the cock was standing by the well, and cried:

> *"Cock-a-doodle-doo!*
> *Your Golden Girl's came back to you!"*

So she went into her mother. And as she was thus covered with gold, she was welcomed by both her and the sister.

The girl told all that had happened to her. As soon as the mother heard how she had come by such great riches, she was anxious for the same good fortune to befall her ugly and lazy daughter. She had to seat herself by the well and spin. And in order that her shuttle might be stained with blood, she stuck her hand into a thorn-bush, and pricked her finger. Then she threw her shuttle into the well, and jumped in after it.

She came like the other to the beautiful meadow, and walked along the very same path. When she got to the oven, the bread cried again:

> *"Oh, take me out! Take me out!*
> *Or I shall burn. I am well baked!"*

But the lazy thing answered, "As if I wanted to soil myself!" and on she went.

Soon she came to the apple-tree, which cried:

"Oh, shake me! Shake me!
We apples are all ripe!"

But she answered, "I like that! One of you might fall on my head!" and on she went.

When she came to Mother Holle's house, she was not afraid, for she had already heard about her big teeth. She hired herself out immediately.

The first day, she made herself work diligently, and obeyed Mother Holle, when she told her to do anything, for she was thinking of all the gold that she would give her.

But on the second day, she began to be lazy, and on the third day stall more so, for then she would not get up in the morning. Neither did she make Mother Holle's bed carefully, nor shake it so as to make the feathers fly up.

Mother Holle was soon tired of this, and gave her notice to leave. The lazy girl was willing to go, and thought that now the Gold-Rain would come. Mother Holle led her to the great doorway. But while she was standing under it, instead of gold, a big kettleful of pitch was emptied over her.

"That is the reward of your service," said Mother Holle, and shut the door.

So the lazy girl went home. She was covered with pitch, and the cock by the well, as soon as he saw her, cried out:

"Cock-a-doodle-doo!
Your Pitchy Girl's come back to you!"

But the pitch stuck fast to her, and could not be got off so long as she lived.

THE FROG-PRINCE

One fine evening a young princess put on her bonnet and clogs, and went out to take a walk by herself in a wood; and when she came to a cool spring of water, that rose in the midst of it, she sat herself down to rest a while. Now she had a golden ball in her hand, which was her favourite plaything; and she was always tossing it up into the air, and catching it again as it fell. After a time she threw it up so high that she missed catching it as it fell; and the ball bounded away, and rolled along upon the ground, till at last it fell down into the spring. The princess looked into the spring after her ball, but it was very deep, so deep that she could not see the bottom of it. Then she began to bewail her loss, and said, "Alas! if I could only get my ball again, I would give all my fine clothes and jewels, and everything that I have in the world."

Whilst she was speaking, a frog put its head out of the water, and said, "Princess, why do you weep so bitterly?" "Alas!" said she, "what can you do for me, you nasty frog? My golden ball has fallen into the spring." The frog said, "I want not your pearls, and jewels, and fine clothes; but if you will love me, and let me live with you and eat from off your golden plate, and sleep upon your bed, I will bring you your ball again." "What nonsense," thought the princess, "this silly frog is talking! He can never even get out of the spring to visit me, though he may be able to get my ball for me, and therefore I will tell him he shall have what he asks." So she said to the frog, "Well, if you will bring me my ball, I will do all you ask." Then the frog put his head down, and dived deep under the water; and after a little while he came up again, with the ball in his mouth, and threw it on the edge of the spring. As soon as the young princess saw her ball, she ran to pick it up; and she was so overjoyed to have it in her hand again, that she never thought of the frog, but ran home with it as fast as she could. The frog called after her, "Stay, princess, and take me with you as you said," But she did not stop to hear a word.

The next day, just as the princess had sat down to dinner, she heard a strange noise – tap, tap – plash, plash – as if something was coming up the marble staircase: and soon afterwards there was a gentle knock at the door, and a little voice cried out and said:

> *"Open the door, my princess dear,*
> *Open the door to thy true love here!*
> *And mind the words that thou and I said*
> *By the fountain cool, in the greenwood shade."*

Then the princess ran to the door and opened it, and there she saw the frog, whom she had quite forgotten. At this sight she was sadly frightened, and shutting the door as fast as she could came back to her seat. The king, her father, seeing that something had frightened her, asked her what was the matter. "There is a nasty frog," said she, "at the door, that lifted my ball for me out of the spring this morning: I told him that he should live with me here, thinking that he could never get out of the spring; but there he is at the door, and he wants to come in."

While she was speaking the frog knocked again at the door, and said:

> *"Open the door, my princess dear,*
> *Open the door to thy true love here!*
> *And mind the words that thou and I said*
> *By the fountain cool, in the greenwood shade."*

Then the king said to the young princess, "As you have given your word you must keep it; so go and let him in." She did so, and the frog hopped into the room, and then straight on – tap, tap – plash, plash – from the bottom of the room to the top, till he came up close to the table where the princess sat. "Pray lift me upon chair," said he to the princess, "and let me sit next to you." As soon as she had done this, the frog said, "Put your plate nearer to me, that I may eat out of it." This she did, and when he had eaten as much as he could, he said, "Now I am tired; carry me upstairs, and put me into your bed." And the princess, though very unwilling, took him up in her hand, and put him upon the pillow of her own bed, where he slept all night long. As soon as it was light he jumped up, hopped downstairs, and went out of the house. "Now, then," thought the princess, "at last he is gone, and I shall be troubled with him no more."

But she was mistaken; for when night came again she heard the same tapping at the door; and the frog came once more, and said:

> *"Open the door, my princess dear,*
> *Open the door to thy true love here!*
> *And mind the words that thou and I said*
> *By the fountain cool, in the greenwood shade."*

And when the princess opened the door the frog came in, and slept upon her pillow as before, till the morning broke. And the third night he did the same. But when the princess awoke on the following morning she was astonished to see, instead of the frog, a handsome prince, gazing on her with the most beautiful eyes she had ever seen, and standing at the head of her bed.

He told her that he had been enchanted by a spiteful fairy, who had changed him into a frog; and that he had been fated so to abide till some princess should take him out of the spring, and let him eat from her plate, and sleep upon her bed for three nights. "You," said the prince, "have broken his cruel charm, and now I have nothing to wish for but that you should go with me into my father's kingdom, where I will marry you, and love you as long as you live."

The young princess, you may be sure, was not long in saying "Yes" to all this; and as they spoke a gay coach drove up, with eight beautiful horses, decked with plumes of feathers and a golden harness; and behind the coach rode the prince's servant, faithful Heinrich, who had bewailed the misfortunes of his dear master during his enchantment so long and so bitterly, that his heart had well-nigh burst.

They then took leave of the king, and got into the coach with eight horses, and all set out, full of joy and merriment, for the prince's kingdom, which they reached safely; and there they lived happily a great many years.

THE FISHERMAN
AND HIS WIFE

There was once on a time, a Fisherman who lived with his wife in a miserable hovel close by the sea, and every day he went out fishing. And once, as he was sitting with his rod, looking at the clear water, his line suddenly went down, far down below, and when he drew it up again, he brought out a large Flounder.

Then the Flounder said to him: "Hark, you Fisherman, I pray you, let me live. I am no Flounder really, but an enchanted Prince. What good will it do you to kill me? I should not be good to eat. Put me in the water again, and let me go."

"Come," said the Fisherman, "there is no need for so many words about it – a fish that can talk I should certainly let go, anyhow."

With that he put him back again into the clear water, and the Flounder went to the bottom, leaving a long streak of blood behind him. Then the Fisherman got up and went home to his wife in the hovel.

"Husband," said the woman, "have you caught nothing today?"

"No," said the man, "I did catch a Flounder, who said he was an enchanted Prince, so I let him go again."

"Did you not wish for anything first?" said the woman.

"No," said the man; "what should I wish for?"

"Ah," said the woman, "it is surely hard to have to live always in this dirty hovel. You might have wished for a small cottage for us. Go back and call him. Tell him we want to have a small cottage. He will certainly give us that."

"Ah," said the man, "why should I go there again?"

"Why," said the woman, "you did catch him, and you let him go again. He is sure to do it. Go at once."

The man still did not quite like to go, but did not want to oppose his wife, and went to the sea.

When he got there the sea was all green and yellow, and no longer smooth. So he stood and said:

> *"Flounder, Flounder in the sea,*
> *Come, I pray thee, here to me;*
> *For my wife, Dame Ilsabil,*
> *Wills not as I'd have her will."*

Then the Flounder came swimming to him and said, "Well, what does she want, then?"

"Ah," said the man, "I did catch you, and my wife says I really ought to have wished for something. She does not like to live in a wretched hovel any longer. She would like to have a cottage."

"Go, then," said the Flounder, "she has it already."

When the man got home, his wife was no longer in the hovel. But instead of it, there stood a small cottage, and she was sitting on a bench before the door. Then she took him by the hand and said to him, "Just come inside, look. Now isn't this a great deal better?"

So they went in, and there was a small porch, and a pretty

little parlor and bedroom, and a kitchen and pantry, with the best of furniture, and fitted up with the most beautiful things made of tin and brass, whatsoever was wanted. And behind the cottage, there was a small yard, with hens and ducks, and a little garden with flowers and fruit.

"Look," said the wife, "is not that nice!"

"Yes," said the husband, "and so we must always think it, – now we will live quite contented."

"We will think about that," said the wife.

With that they ate something and went to bed.

Everything went well for a week or a fortnight, and then the woman said, "Hark you, Husband, this cottage is far too small for us, and the garden and yard are little. The Flounder might just as well have given us a larger house. I should like to live in a great stone castle. Go to the Flounder, and tell him to give us a castle."

"Ah, Wife," said the man, "the cottage is quite good enough. Why should we live in a castle?"

"What!" said the woman; "go at once, the Flounder can always do that."

"No, Wife," said the man, "the Flounder has just given us the cottage. I do not like to go back so soon, it might make him angry."

"Go," said the woman, "he can do it quite easily, and will be glad to do it. Just you go to him."

The man's heart grew heavy, and he did not wish to go. He said to himself, "It is not right," and yet he went.

And when he came to the sea, the water was quite purple and dark-blue, and gray and thick, and no longer green and yellow, but it was still quiet. And he stood there and said:

> *"Flounder, Flounder in the sea,*
> *Come, I pray thee, here to me;*
> *For my wife, Dame Ilsabil,*
> *Wills not as I'd have her will."*

"Well, what does she want, now?" said the Flounder.

"Alas," said the man, half scared, "she wants to live in a great stone castle."

"Go to it, then, she is standing before the door," said the Flounder.

Then the man went home, and when he got there, he found a great stone palace, and his wife was just standing on the steps going in. She took him by the hand and said, "Come in."

So he went with her, and in the castle was a great hall paved with marble, and many servants, who flung wide the doors. The walls were all bright with beautiful hangings, and in the rooms were chairs and tables of pure gold. Crystal chandeliers hung from the ceiling, and all the rooms and bedrooms had carpets. Food and wine of the very best were standing on all the tables, so that they nearly broke down beneath it.

Behind the house, too, there was a great courtyard, with stables for horses and cows, and the very best of carriages. There was a magnificent large garden, too, with the most beautiful flowers and fruit-trees, and a park quite half a mile long, in which were stags, deer, and hares, and everything that could be desired.

"Come," said the woman, "isn't that beautiful?"

"Yes, indeed," said the man, "now let it be; and we will live in this beautiful castle and be content."

"We will consider about that," said the woman, "and sleep upon it;" thereupon they went to bed.

Next morning, the wife awoke first. It was just daybreak, and from her bed she saw the beautiful country lying before her. Her husband was still stretching himself, so she poked him in the side with her elbow, and said, "Get up, Husband, and just peep out of the window. Look you, couldn't we be the King over all that land? Go to the Flounder, we will be the King."

"Ah, Wife," said the man, "why should we be King? I do not want to be King."

"Well," said the wife, "if you won't be King, I will. Go to the Flounder, for I will be King."

"Ah, Wife," said the man, "why do you want to be King? I do not like to say that to him."

"Why not?" said the woman; "go to him at once. I must be King!"

So the man went, and was quite unhappy because his wife wished to be King. "It is not right; it is not right," thought he. He did not wish to go, but yet he went.

And when he came to the sea, it was quite dark-gray, and the water heaved up from below, and smelt putrid. Then he went and stood by it, and said:

> *"Flounder, Flounder in the sea,*
> *Come, I pray thee, here to me;*
> *For my wife, Dame Ilsabil,*
> *Wills not as I'd have her will."*

"Well, what does she want, now?" said the Flounder.

"Alas," said the man, "she wants to be King."

"Go to her; she is King already."

So the man went, and when he came to the palace, the castle had become much larger, and had a great tower and magnificent ornaments. The sentinel was standing before the door, and there were numbers of soldiers with kettledrums and trumpets. And when he went inside the house, everything was of real marble and gold, with velvet covers and great golden tassels. Then the doors of the hall were opened, and there was the Court in all its splendor, and his wife was sitting on a high throne of gold and diamonds, with a great crown of gold on her head, and a sceptre of pure gold and jewels in her hand. On both sides of her, stood her maids-in-waiting in a row, each of them always one head shorter than the last.

Then he went and stood before her, and said, "Ah, Wife, and now you are King."

"Yes," said the woman, "now I am King."

So he stood and looked at her, and when he had looked at her thus for some time, he said, "And now that you are King, let all else be, we will wish for nothing more."

"Nay, Husband," said the woman, quite anxiously, "I find time pass very heavily, I can bear it no longer. Go to the Flounder – I am King, but I must be Emperor, too."

"Alas, Wife, why do you wish to be Emperor?"

"Husband," said she, "go to the Flounder. I will be Emperor."

"Alas, Wife," said the man, "he cannot make you Emperor. I may not say that to the fish. There is only one Emperor in the land. An Emperor, the Flounder cannot make you! I assure you he cannot."

"What!" said the woman, "I am the King, and you are nothing but my husband. Will you go this moment? go at once! If he can make a King, he can make an Emperor. I will be Emperor. Go instantly."

So he was forced to go. As the man went, however, he was troubled in mind, and thought to himself, "It will not end well! It will not end well! Emperor is too shameless! The Flounder will at last be tired out."

With that, he reached the sea, and the sea was quite black and thick, and began to boil up from below, so that it threw up bubbles. And such a sharp wind blew over it that it curdled, and the man was afraid. Then he went and stood by it, and said:

> "*Flounder, Flounder in the sea,*
> *Come, I pray thee, here to me;*
> *For my wife, Dame Ilsabil,*
> *Wills not as I'd have her will.*"

"Well, what does she want, now?" said the Flounder.

"Alas, Flounder," said he, "my wife wants to be Emperor."

"Go to her," said the Flounder; "she is Emperor already."

So the man went, and when he got there the whole palace

was made of polished marble with alabaster figures and golden ornaments. And soldiers were marching before the door blowing trumpets, and beating cymbals and drums. In the house, barons, and counts, and dukes were going about as servants. Then they opened the doors to him, which were of pure gold. And when he entered, there sat his wife on a throne, which was made of one piece of gold, and was quite two miles high; and she wore a great golden crown that was three yards high, and set with diamonds and carbuncles. In one hand she had the sceptre, and in the other the imperial orb. And on both sides of her stood the yeomen of the guard in two rows, each being smaller than the one before him, from the biggest Giant, who was two miles high, to the very smallest Dwarf, just as big as my little finger. And before it stood a number of princes and dukes.

Then the man went and stood among than, and said, "Wife, are you Emperor now?"

"Yes," said she, "now I am Emperor."

Then he stood and looked at her well, and when he had looked at her thus for some time, he said, "Ah, Wife, be content, now that you are Emperor."

"Husband," said she, "why are you standing there? Now, I am Emperor, but I will be Pope too. Go to the Flounder."

"Alas, Wife," said the man, "what will you not wish for? You cannot be Pope. There is but one in Christendom. He cannot make you Pope."

"Husband," said she, "I will be Pope. Go immediately. I must be Pope this very day." "No, Wife," said the man, "I do not like to say that to him; that would not do, it is too much. The Flounder can't make you Pope."

"Husband," said she, "what nonsense! if he can make an Emperor he can make a Pope. Go to him directly. I am Emperor, and you are nothing but my husband. Will you go at once?"

Then he was afraid and went. But he was quite faint, and shivered and shook, and his knees and legs trembled. And a high wind blew over the land, and the clouds flew, and toward evening all grew dark, and the leaves fell from the trees, and the water rose and roared as if it were boiling, and splashed upon the shore. In the distance he saw ships which were firing guns in their sore need, pitching and tossing on the waves. And yet in the midst of the sky, there was still a small bit of blue, though on every side it was as red as in a heavy storm. So, full of despair, he went and stood in much fear, and said:

> *"Flounder, Flounder in the sea,*
> *Come, I pray thee, here to me;*
> *For my wife, Dame Ilsabil,*
> *Wills not as I'd have her will."*

"Well, what does she want, now?" said the Flounder.

"Alas," said the man, "she wants to be Pope."

"Go to her then," said the Flounder; "she is Pope already."

So he went, and when he got there, he saw what seemed to be a large church surrounded by palaces. He pushed his way through the crowd. Inside, however, everything was lighted with thousands and thousands of candles, and his wife was clad in gold, and she was sitting on a much higher throne, and had three great golden crowns on, and round about her there was much churchly splendor. And on both sides of her was a row of candles, the largest of which was as tall as the very tallest tower, down to the very smallest kitchen candle; and all the emperors and kings were on their knees before her, kissing her shoe.

"Wife," said the man, and looked attentively at her, "are you now Pope?"

"Yes," said she, "I am Pope."

So he stood and looked at her, and it was just as if he was looking at the bright sun. When he had stood looking at her thus for a short time, he said, "Ah, Wife, if you are Pope, do let well alone!"

But she looked as stiff as a post, and did not move or show

any signs of life. Then said he, "Wife, now that you are Pope, be satisfied, you cannot become anything greater."

"I will consider about that," said the woman.

Thereupon they both went to bed. But she was not satisfied, and greediness let her have no sleep, for she was continually thinking what there was left for her to be.

The man slept well and soundly, for he had run about a great deal during the day. But the woman could not fall asleep at all, and flung herself from one side to the other the whole night through, thinking what more was left for her to be, but unable to call to mind anything else.

At length the sun began to rise, and when the woman saw the red of dawn, she sat up in bed and looked at it. And when, through the window, she saw the sun thus rising, she said, "Cannot I, too, order the sun and moon to rise?"

"Husband," said she, poking him in the ribs with her elbows, "wake up! go to the Flounder, for I wish to be even as God is."

The man was still half asleep, but he was so horrified that he fell out of bed. He thought he must have heard amiss, and rubbed his eyes, and said, "Alas, Wife, what are you saying?"

"Husband," said she, "if I can't order the sun and moon to rise, and have to look on and see the sun and moon rising, I can't bear it. I shall not know what it is to have another happy hour, unless I can make them rise myself." Then she looked at him so terribly that a shudder ran over him, and said, "Go at once. I wish to be like unto God."

"Alas, Wife," said the man, falling on his knees before her, "the Flounder cannot do that. He can make an Emperor and a Pope. I beseech you, go on as you are, and be Pope."

Then she fell into a rage, and her hair flew wildly about her head, and she cried, "I will not endure this, I'll not bear it any longer. Will you go?" Then he put on his trousers and ran away like a madman.

But outside a great storm was raging, and blowing so hard that he could scarcely keep his feet. Houses and trees toppled over, mountains trembled, rocks rolled into the sea, the sky was pitch black, and it thundered and lightened. And the sea came in with black waves as high as church-towers and mountains, and all with crests of white foam at the top. Then he cried, but could not hear his own words:

> "*Flounder, Flounder in the sea,*
> *Come, I pray thee, here to me;*
> *For my wife, Dame Ilsabil,*
> *Wills not as I'd have her will.*"

"Well; what does she want, now?" said the Flounder.

"Alas," said he, "she wants to be like unto God."

"Go to her, and you will find her back again in the dirty hovel."

And there they are living at this very time.

SNOW-WHITE AND ROSE-RED

There was once a poor widow who lived in a lonely cottage. In front of the cottage was a garden wherein stood two rose-trees, one of which bore white and the other red roses. She had two children who were like the two rose-trees. One was called Snow-White, and the other Rose-Red.

They were as good and happy, as busy and cheerful as ever two children in the world were, only Snow-White was more quiet and gentle than Rose-Red. Rose-Red liked better to run about in the meadows and fields seeking flowers and catching butterflies. But Snow-White sat at home with her mother, and helped her with the housework, or read to her when there was nothing to do.

The two children were so fond of each other, that they always held each other by the hand when they went out together. When Snow-White said, "We will not leave each other," Rose-Red answered, "Never so long as we live." And their mother would add, "What one has, she must share with the other."

They often ran about the forest alone and gathered red berries. Beasts never did them any harm, but came close to them trustfully. The little hare would eat a cabbage-leaf out of their hands, the roe grazed by their side, the stag leapt merrily by them, and the birds sat still upon the boughs, and sang whatever they knew.

No mishap overtook them. If they stayed too late in the forest, and night came on, they laid themselves down near one another upon the moss, and slept until morning. Their mother knew this, and had no worry on their account.

One day, when they had spent the night in the wood and the dawn had roused them, they saw a beautiful Child in a shining white dress sitting near their bed. He got up and looked quite kindly at them, but said nothing and went away into the forest. And when they looked round, they found that they had been sleeping quite close to a precipice, and would certainly have fallen into it in the darkness, if they had gone only a few paces farther. And their mother told them that it must have been the Angel who watches over good children.

Snow-White and Rose-Red kept their mother's little cottage so neat, that it was a pleasure to look inside it. In the summer, Rose-Red took care of the house, and every morning laid a wreath of flowers by her mother's bed before she awoke, in which was a rose from each tree. In the winter, Snow-White lit the fire and hung the kettle on the hook. The kettle was of copper and shone like gold, so brightly was it polished.

In the evening, when the snowflakes fell, the mother said, "Go, Snow-White, and bolt the door," and then they sat round the hearth, and the mother took her spectacles and read aloud out of a large book. The two girls listened as they sat and span. And close by them lay a lamb upon the floor, and behind them upon a perch sat a white dove with its head hidden beneath its wings.

One evening, as they were thus sitting comfortably together, some one knocked at the door as if he wished to be let in. The mother said, "Quick, Rose-Red, open the door, it must be a traveler who is seeking shelter."

Rose-Red went and pushed back the bolt, thinking that it was a poor man, but it was not. It was a Bear that stretched his broad, black head within the door.

Rose-Red screamed and sprang back, the lamb bleated, the dove fluttered, and Snow-White hid herself behind her mother's bed.

But the Bear began to speak and said, "Do not be afraid. I will do you no harm! I am half-frozen, and only want to warm myself a little beside you."

"Poor Bear," said the mother, "lie down by the fire. Only take care that you do not burn your coat." Then she cried, "Snow-White, Rose-Red, come out, the Bear will do you no harm, he means well."

So they both came out, and by-and-by the lamb and dove came nearer, and were not afraid of him.

The Bear said, "Here, Children, knock the snow out of my coat a little;" so they brought the broom and swept the Bear's hide clean. And he stretched himself by the fire and growled contentedly and comfortably.

It was not long before they grew quite at home, and played tricks with their clumsy guest. They tugged at his hair with their hands, put their feet upon his back and rolled him about, or they took a hazel-switch and beat him, and, when he growled, they laughed. But the Bear took it all in good part, only when they were too rough he called out, "Leave me alive, Children:

> *"Snowy-white, Rosy-red,*
> *Will you beat your lover dead?"*

When it was bedtime, and the others went to sleep, the mother said to the Bear, "You may lie there by the hearth, and then you will be safe from the cold and the bad weather."

As soon as day dawned the two children let him out, and he trotted across the snow into the forest.

Henceforth the Bear came every evening at the same time, laid himself down by the hearth, and let the children amuse themselves with him as much as they liked. They got so used to him, that the doors were never fastened until their black friend had arrived.

When spring was come and all outside was green, the Bear said one morning to Snow-White, "Now I must go away, and cannot come back for the whole summer."

"Where are you going, then, dear Bear?" asked Snow-White.

"I must go into the forest and guard my treasures from the wicked Dwarfs. In the winter, when the earth is frozen hard, they are obliged to stay below and cannot work their way through. But now, when the sun has thawed and warmed the earth, they break through it, and come out to pry and steal. And what once gets into their hands and in their caves, does not easily see daylight again."

Snow-White was very sorry for his going away. And as she unbolted the door for him, and the Bear was hurrying out, he caught against the bolt and a piece of his hairy coat was torn off. It seemed to Snow-White as if she saw gold shining through it, but she was not sure about it. The Bear ran away quickly, and was soon out of sight behind the trees.

A short time afterward, the mother sent her children into the forest to get fire-wood. There they found a big tree which lay felled on the ground, and close by the trunk something was jumping backward and forward in the grass. But they could not make out what it was.

When they came nearer they saw a Dwarf with an old withered face and a snow-white beard a yard long. The end of the beard was caught in a crevice of the tree, and the little fellow was jumping backward and forward like a dog tied to a rope, and did not know what to do.

He glared at the girls with his fiery red eyes and cried, "Why do you stand there? Can you not come here and help me?"

"What are you about there, Little Man?" asked Rose-Red.

"You stupid, prying goose!" answered the Dwarf; "I was

going to split the tree to get a little wood for cooking. The little bit of food that one of us wants gets burnt up directly with thick logs. We do not swallow so much as you coarse, greedy folk. I had just driven the wedge safely in, and everything was going as I wished; but the wretched wood was too smooth and suddenly sprang asunder, and the tree closed so quickly that I could not pull out my beautiful white beard. So now it is tight in, and I cannot get away. And you silly, sleek, milk-faced things laugh! Ugh! how odious you are!"

The children tried very hard, but they could not pull the beard out, it was caught too fast.

"I will run and fetch some one," said Rose-Red.

"You senseless goose!" snarled the Dwarf. "Why should you fetch some one? You are already two too many for me. Can you not think of something better?"

"Don't be impatient," said Snow-White, "I will help you," and she pulled her scissors out of her pocket, and cut off the end of the beard.

As soon as the Dwarf felt himself free, he grabbed a bag which lay amongst the roots of the tree, and which was full of gold, and lifted it up, grumbling to himself, "Rude people, to cut off a piece of my fine beard! Bad luck to you!" and then he swung the bag upon his back, and went off without even once looking at the children.

Some time after that Snow-White and Rose-Red went to catch a dish of fish. As they came near the brook, they saw something like a large grasshopper jumping toward the water, as if it were going to leap in. They ran to it and found it was the Dwarf.

"Where are you going?" said Rose-Red; "you surely don't want to go into the water?"

"I am not such a fool!" cried the Dwarf; "don't you see that the accursed fish wants to pull me in?" The Little Man had been sitting there fishing, and unluckily the wind had twisted his beard with the fishing-line. Just then a big fish bit, and the feeble creature had not strength to pull it out. The fish kept the upper hand and was pulling the Dwarf toward him. He held on to all the reeds and rushes, but it was of little good, he was forced to follow the fish, and was in great danger of being dragged into the water.

The girls came just in time. They held him fast and tried to free his beard from the line. But all in vain, beard and line were entangled fast together. Nothing was left but to bring out the scissors and cut the beard, whereby a small part of it was lost.

When the Dwarf saw that, he screamed out, "Is that civil, you toadstool, to disfigure one's face? Was it not enough to clip off the end of my beard? Now you have cut off the best part of it. I cannot let myself be seen by my people. I wish you had been made to run the soles off your shoes!" Then he took out a sack of pearls which lay in the rushes, and, without saying a word more, he dragged it away and disappeared behind a stone.

It happened that soon afterward the mother sent the two children to the town to buy needles and thread, and laces and ribbons. The road led them across a heath upon which huge pieces of rock lay strewn about. They now noticed a large bird hovering in the air, flying slowly round and round above them. It sank lower and lower, and at last settled near a rock not far off. Directly afterward they heard a loud, piteous cry. They ran up and saw, with horror, that the eagle had seized their old acquaintance the Dwarf, and was going to carry him off.

The children, full of pity, at once took tight hold of the Little Man, and pulled against the eagle so long that at last he let his booty go.

As soon as the Dwarf had recovered from his first fright, he cried with his shrill voice, "Could you not have done it more carefully! You dragged at my brown coat, so that it is all torn and full of holes. You helpless, clumsy creatures!" Then he took up a sack full of precious stones, and slipped away again under the rock into his hole.

The girls, who by this time were used to his thanklessness, went on their way and did their business in the town.

As they crossed the heath again on their way home they surprised the Dwarf, who had emptied out his bag of precious stones in a clean spot, and had not thought that any one would come there at such a late hour. The evening sun shone upon the brilliant stones. They glittered and sparkled with all colors so beautifully, that the children stood still and looked at them.

"Why do you stand gaping there?" cried the Dwarf, and his ashen-gray face became copper-red with rage. He was going on with his bad words, when a loud growling was heard, and a black Bear came trotting toward them out of the forest. The Dwarf sprang up in a fright, but he could not get to his cave, for the Bear was already close.

Then in the fear of his heart he cried, "Dear Mr. Bear, spare me! I will give you all my treasures! Look, the beautiful jewels lying there! Grant me my life. What do you want with such a slender little fellow as I? You would not feel me between your teeth. Come, take these two wicked girls, they are tender morsels for you, fat as young quails. For mercy's sake eat them!"

The Bear took no heed of his words, but gave the wicked creature a single blow with his paw, and he did not move again.

The girls had run away, but the Bear called to them, "Snow-White and Rose-Red, do not be afraid. Wait, I will come with you."

Then they knew his voice and waited. And when he came up to them, suddenly his bear-skin fell off, and he stood there a handsome man, clothed all in gold.

"I am a King's Son," he said, "and I was bewitched by that wicked Dwarf, who had stolen my treasures. I have had to run about the forest as a savage bear until I was freed by his death. Now he has got his well-deserved punishment."

Snow-White was married to him, and Rose-Red to his brother. They divided between them the great treasure which the Dwarf had gathered together in his cave. The old mother lived peacefully and happily with her children for many years. She took the two rose-trees with her, and they stood before her window, and every year bore the most beautiful roses, white and red.

RUMPELSTILTSKIN

Once there was a miller who was poor, but who had a beautiful daughter. Now it happened that he had to speak to the King, and in order to make himself appear important he said to him, "I have a daughter who can spin straw into gold."

The King said to the miller, "That is an art which pleases me well. If your daughter is as clever as you say, bring her tomorrow to my palace, and I will try what she can do."

And when the girl was brought to him, he took her into a room which was quite full of straw, gave her a spinning-wheel and a reel, and said, "Now set to work. If by tomorrow morning early, you have not spun this straw into gold, you must die."

Thereupon he himself locked up the room, and left her in it alone. So there sat the poor miller's daughter, and for her life could not tell what to do. She had no idea how straw could be spun into gold; and she grew more and more miserable, until at last she began to weep.

But all at once the door opened, and in came a Little Man, and said, "Good evening, Mistress Miller. Why are you crying so?"

"Alas!" answered the girl, "I have to spin straw into gold, and I do not know how to do it."

"What will you give me," said the Little Man, "if I do it for you?"

"My necklace," said the girl.

The Little Man took the necklace, seated himself in front of the wheel, and *whirr, whirr, whirr,* three turns, and the reel was full. Then he put another on, and *whirr, whirr, whirr,* three times round, and the second was full too. And so it went on till the morning, when all the straw was spun, and all the reels were full of gold.

By daybreak, the King was there, and when he saw the gold, he was astonished and delighted, but his heart became only more greedy. He had the miller's daughter taken into another room full of straw, which was much larger, and commanded her to spin that also in one night if she valued her life.

The girl knew not how to help herself, and was crying, when the door again opened, and the Little Man appeared, and said, "What will you give me if I spin the straw into gold for you?"

"The ring on my finger," answered the girl.

The Little Man took the ring, again began to turn the wheel, and, by morning, had spun all the straw into glittering gold.

The King rejoiced beyond measure at the sight, but still he had not gold enough. He had the miller's daughter taken into a still larger room full of straw, and said, "You must spin this, too, in the course of this night. But if you succeed, you shall be my wife." "Even if she be a miller's daughter," thought he, "I could not find a richer wife in the whole world."

When the girl was alone the Little Man came again for the third time, and said, "What will you give me if I spin the straw for you this time also?"

"I have nothing left that I could give," answered the girl.

"Then promise me, if you should become Queen, your first child."

"Who knows whether that will ever happen?" thought the miller's daughter. And, not knowing how else to help herself in this difficulty, she promised the Little Man what he wanted. And for that he once more span the straw into gold.

And when the King came in the morning, and found all as he had wished, he took her in marriage. And the pretty miller's daughter became a Queen.

A year after, she had a beautiful child, and she never gave a thought to the Little Man. But suddenly he came into her room, and said, "Now give me what you promised."

The Queen was horror-struck, and offered the Little Man all the riches of the kingdom if he would leave her the child.

But the Little Man said, "No, something that is alive, is dearer to me than all the treasures in the world."

Then the Queen began to weep and cry, so that the Little Man pitied her. "I will give you three days' time," said he; "if by that time you find out my name, then you shall keep your child."

So the Queen thought the whole night of all the names that she had ever heard, and she sent a messenger over the country to inquire, far and wide, for any other names there might be.

When the Little Man came the next day, she began with *Caspar, Melchior, Balthazar,* and said all the names she knew, one after another. But to every one the Little Man said, "That is not my name."

On the second day, she had inquiries made in the neighborhood as to the names of the people there. And she repeated to the Little Man the most uncommon and curious, "Perhaps your name is *Shortribs*, or *Sheepshanks*, or *Laceleg*?" but he always answered, "That is not my name."

On the third day, the messenger came back again, and said, "I have not been able to find a single new name. But as I came to a high mountain at the end of the forest, where the fox and the hare bid each other good night, there I saw a little house. Before the house a fire was burning, and round about the fire a funny Little Man was jumping. He hopped upon one leg, and shouted:

> *"Today I brew, tomorrow I bake,*
> *And next, I shall the Queen's child take!*
> *Ah! well it is, none knows the same –*
> *That Rumpelstiltskin is my name!"*

You may think how glad the Queen was when she heard the name! And when soon afterward the Little Man came in, and asked, "Now, Mistress Queen, what is my name?" she said:

"Is your name *Conrad*?"

"No."

"Is your name *Harry*?"

"No."

"Perhaps your name is *Rumpelstiltskin*?"

"The devil has told you that! the devil has told you that!" cried the Little Man, and in his anger he stamped his right foot so deep into the earth that his whole leg went in. And then in rage, he pulled at his left leg so hard with both hands, that he tore himself in two.

CINDERELLA

The wife of a rich man fell sick: and when she felt that her end drew nigh, she called her only daughter to her bedside, and said, "Always be a good girl, and I will look down from heaven and watch over you." Soon afterwards she shut her eyes and died, and was buried in the garden; and the little girl went every day to her grave and wept, and was always good and kind to all about her. And the snow spread a beautiful white covering over the grave; but by the time the sun had melted it away again, her father had married another wife. This new wife had two daughters of her own: they were fair in face but foul at heart, and it was now a sorry time for the poor little girl. "What does the good-for-nothing thing want in the parlor?" said they; and they took away her fine clothes, and gave her an old frock to put on, and laughed at her and turned her into the kitchen.

Then she was forced to do hard work; to rise early, before daylight, to bring the water, to make the fire, to cook and to wash. She had no bed to lie down on, but was made to lie by the hearth among the ashes, and they called her Cinderella.

It happened once that her father was going to the fair, and asked his wife's daughters what he should bring to them.

"Fine clothes," said the first. "Pearls and diamonds," said the second. "Now, child," said he to his own daughter, "what will you have?" "The first sprig, dear father, that rubs against your hat on your way home," said she. Then he bought for the two first the fine clothes and pearls and diamonds they had asked for: and on his way home, as he rode through a green copse, a sprig of hazel brushed against him, so he broke it off and when he got home he gave it to his daughter. Then she took it, and went to her mother's grave and planted it there, and cried so much that it was watered with her tears; and there it grew and became a fine tree, and soon a little bird came and built its nest upon the tree, and talked with her and watched over her, and brought her whatever she wished for.

Now it happened that the king of the land held a feast which was to last three days, and out of those who came to it his son was to choose a bride for himself; and Cinderella's two sisters were asked to come. So they called Cinderella, and said, "Now, comb our hair, brush our shoes, and tie our sashes for us, for we are going to dance at the king's feast." Then she did as she was told, but when all was done she could not help crying, for she thought to herself, she would have liked to go to the dance too, and at last she begged her mother very hard to let her go, "You! Cinderella?" said she; "you who have nothing to wear, no clothes at all, and who cannot even dance – you want to go to the ball?" And when she kept on begging, to get rid of her, she said at last, "I will throw this basinful of peas into the ash heap, and if you have picked them all out in two hours' time you shall go to the feast too."

Then she threw the peas into the ashes; but the little maiden ran out at the back door into the garden, and cried out:

> "Hither, thither, through the sky, turtle-
> doves and linnets, fly!
> Blackbird, thrush, and chaffinch gay, hither,
> thither, haste away!

One and all, come, help me quick! haste ye,
haste ye – pick, pick, pick!"

Then first came two white doves; and next two turtle-doves; and after them all the little birds under heaven came, and the little doves stooped their heads down and set to work, pick, pick, pick; and then the others began to pick, pick, pick, and picked out all the good grain and put it into a dish, and left the ashes. At the end of one hour the work was done, and all flew out again at the windows. Then she brought the dish to her mother. But the mother said, "No, no! indeed, you have no clothes and cannot dance; you shall not go." And when Cinderella begged very hard to go, she said, "If you can in one hour's time pick two of these dishes of pease out of the ashes, you shall go too." So she shook two dishes of peas into the ashes; but the little maiden went out into the garden at the back of the house, and called as before and all the birds came flying, and in half an hour's time all was done, and out they flew again. And then Cinderella took the dishes to her mother, rejoicing to think that she should now go to the ball. But her mother said, "It is all of no use, you cannot go; you have no clothes, and cannot dance; and you would only put us to shame;" and off she went with her two daughters to the feast.

Now when all were gone, and nobody left at home, Cinderella went sorrowfully and sat down under the hazel-tree, and cried out:

"Shake, shake, hazel-tree, gold and silver
over me!"

Then her friend the bird flew out of the tree and brought a gold and silver dress for her, and slippers of spangled silk; and she put them on, and followed her sisters to the feast. But they did not know her, she looked so fine and beautiful in her rich clothes.

The king's son soon came up to her, and took her by the

hand and danced with her and no one else; and he never left her hand, but when any one else came to ask her to dance, he said, "This lady is dancing with me." Thus they danced till a late hour of the night, and then she wanted to go home; and the king's son said, "I shall go and take care of you to your home," for he wanted to see where the beautiful maid lived. But she slipped away from him unawares, and ran off towards home, and the prince followed her; then she jumped up into the pigeon-house and shut the door. So he waited till her father came home, and told him that the unknown maiden who had been at the feast had hidden herself in the pigeon-house. But when they had broken open the door they found no one within; and as they came back into the house, Cinderella lay, as she always did, in her dirty frock by the ashes; for she had run as quickly as she could through the pigeon-house and on to the hazel-tree, and had there taken off her beautiful clothes, and laid them beneath the tree, that the bird might carry them away; and had seated herself amid the ashes again in her little old frock.

The next day, when the feast was again held, and her father, mother and sisters were gone, Cinderella went to the hazel-tree, and all happened as the evening before.

The king's son, who was waiting for her, took her by the hand and danced with her; and, when any one asked her to dance, he said as before, "This lady is dancing with me." When night came she wanted to go home; and the king's son went with her, but she sprang away from him all at once into the garden behind her father's house. In this garden stood a fine large pear-tree; and Cinderella jumped up into it without being seen. Then the king's son waited till her father came home, and said to him, "The unknown lady has slipped away, and I think she must have sprung into the pear-tree." The father ordered an axe to be brought, and they cut down the tree, but found no one upon it. And when they came back into the kitchen, there lay Cinderella in the ashes as usual; for she had slipped down on the other side of the tree, and carried her beautiful clothes back to the bird at the hazel-tree, and then put on her little old frock.

The third day, when her father and mother and sisters were gone, she went again into the garden, and said:

> *"Shake, shake, hazel-tree, gold and silver*
> *over me!"*

Then her kind friend the bird brought a dress still finer than the former one, and slippers which were all of gold; and the king's son danced with her alone, and when any one else asked her to dance, he said, "This lady is my partner." Now when night came she wanted to go home; and the king's son would go with her, but she managed to slip away from him, though in such a hurry that she dropped her left golden slipper upon the stairs.

So the prince took the shoe, and went the next day to the king, his father, and said, "I will take for my wife the lady that this golden shoe fits."

Then both the sisters were overjoyed to hear this; for they had beautiful feet, and had no doubt that they could wear the golden slipper. The eldest went first into the room where the slipper was, and wanted to try it on, and the mother stood by. But her big toe could not go into it, and the shoe was altogether much too small for her. Then the mother said, "Never mind, cut it off. When you are queen you will not care about toes; you will not want to go on foot." So the silly girl cut her big toe off, and squeezed the shoe on, and went to the king's son. Then he took her for his bride, and rode away with her.

But on their way home they had to pass by the hazel-tree that Cinderella had planted, and there sat a little dove on the branch, singing:

> *"Back again! back again! look to the shoe!*
> *The shoe is too small, and not made for you!*

Prince! prince! look again for thy bride,
For she's not the true one that sits by thy side."

Then the prince looked at her foot, and saw by the blood that streamed from it what a trick she had played him. So he brought the false bride back to her home, and said, "This is not the right bride; let the other sister try and put on the slipper." Then she went into the room and got her foot into the shoe, all but the heel, which was too large. But her mother squeezed it in till the blood came, and took her to the king's son; and he rode away with her. But when they came to the hazel-tree, the little dove sat there still, and sang as before. Then the king's son looked down, and saw that the blood streamed from the shoe. So he brought her back again also. "This is not the true bride," said he to the father; "have you no other daughters?"

Then Cinderella came and she took her clumsy shoe off, and put on the golden slipper, and it fitted as if it had been made for her. And when he drew near and looked at her face the prince knew her, and said, "This is the right bride."

Then he took Cinderella on his horse and rode away. And when they came to the hazel-tree the white dove sang:

"Prince! prince! take home thy bride,
For she is the true one that sits by thy side!"

LITTLE RED-CAP

Once upon a time, there was a sweet little girl, who was loved by every one who looked at her, and most of all by her Grandmother. There was nothing that she would not have given the child!

Once she gave her a little cap of red velvet, which suited her so well that she would not wear anything else. So she was always called Little Red-Cap.

One day, her Mother said to her, "Come, Little Red-Cap, here is a piece of cake and a bottle of wine. Take them to your Grandmother. She is ill and weak, and they will do her good. Set out before it gets hot. Walk nicely and quietly. Do not run off the path, or you may fall and break the bottle; then your Grandmother will get nothing! When you go into her room, don't forget to say 'Good morning,' and don't stop to peep into every corner, before you do it."

"I'll take great care," said Little Red-Cap to her Mother, and gave her hand on it.

The Grandmother lived in the wood, half an hour's distance from the village, and just as Little Red-Cap entered the wood, a Wolf met her. Red-Cap did not know what a wicked creature he was, and was not at all afraid of him.

"Good-day, Little Red-Cap," said he.

"Thank you kindly, Wolf."

"Whither away so early, Little Red-Cap?"

"To my Grandmother's."

"What have you got in your apron?"

"Cake and wine. Yesterday was baking-day, so poor sick Grandmother is to have something good, to make her stronger."

"Where does your Grandmother live, Little Red-Cap?"

"A good quarter of an hour farther on in the wood. Her house stands under the three large oak-trees; the nut-trees are just below. You surely must know it," replied Little Red-Cap.

The Wolf thought to himself, "What a tender young creature! what a nice plump mouthful – she will be better to eat than the old woman. I must act craftily, so as to catch both."

He walked for a short time by the side of Little Red-Cap, and then he said, "See, Little Red-Cap, how pretty the flowers are about here – why do you not look round? I believe, too, that you do not hear how sweetly the little birds are singing. You walk gravely along as if you were going to school, while everything else in the wood is merry."

Little Red-Cap raised her eyes, and when she saw the sunbeams dancing here and there through the trees, and pretty flowers growing everywhere, she thought, "Suppose I take Grandmother a fresh nosegay. That would please her too. It is so early in the day that I shall still get there in good time."

And so she ran from the path into the wood to look for flowers. And whenever she had picked one, she fancied that she saw a still prettier one farther on, and ran after it, and thus got deeper and deeper into the wood.

Meanwhile, the Wolf ran straight to the Grandmother's house and knocked at the door.

"Who is there?"

"Little Red-Cap," replied the Wolf. "She is bringing cake and wine. Open the door."

"Lift the latch," called out the Grandmother, "I am too weak, and cannot get up."

The Wolf lifted the latch, the door flew open, and without saying a word he went straight to the Grandmother's bed, and devoured her. Then he put on her clothes, dressed himself in her cap, laid himself in bed, and drew the curtains.

Little Red-Cap, however, had been running about picking flowers. When she had gathered so many that she could carry no more, she remembered her Grandmother, and set out on the way to her.

She was surprised to find the cottage-door standing open. And when she went into the room, she had such a strange feeling, that she said to herself, "Oh dear! how uneasy I feel today, and at other times I like being with Grandmother so much."

She called out, "Good morning," but received no answer. So she went to the bed and drew back the curtains. There lay her Grandmother with her cap pulled far over her face, and looking very strange.

"Oh! Grandmother," she said, "what big ears you have!"

"The better to hear you with, my Child," was the reply.

"But, Grandmother, what big eyes you have!" she said.

"The better to see you with, my dear."

"But, Grandmother, what large hands you have!"

"The better to hug you with."

"Oh! but Grandmother, what a terrible big mouth you have!"

"The better to eat you with!" And scarcely had the Wolf said this, than with one bound he was out of bed and swallowed up Red-Cap.

When the Wolf had satisfied his appetite, he lay down again in the bed, fell asleep and began to snore very loud. The huntsman was just passing the house, and thought to himself, "How the old woman is snoring! I must just see if she wants anything."

So he went into the room, and when he came to the bed, he

saw the Wolf lying in it. "Do I find thee here, thou old sinner!" said he. "I have long sought thee!"

Then just as he was going to fire at him, it occurred to him that the Wolf might have devoured the grandmother, and that she might still be saved. So he did not fire, but took a pair of scissors, and began to cut open the stomach of the sleeping Wolf.

When he had made two snips, he saw the little Red-Cap shining, and then he made two snips more, and the little girl sprang out, crying, "Ah, how frightened I have been! How dark it was inside the Wolf!"

And after that the aged grandmother came out alive also, but scarcely able to breathe.

Red-Cap then quickly fetched great stones with which they filled the Wolf's body. And when he awoke, he wanted to run away, but the stones were so heavy that he tumbled down at once, and fell dead.

Then all three were delighted. The huntsman drew off the Wolf's skin and went home with it. The grandmother ate the cake and drank the wine which Red-Cap had brought, and grew strong again.

But Red-Cap thought to herself, "As long as I live, I will never leave the path to run into the wood, when my mother has forbidden me to do so."

THE JUNIPER-TREE

Long, long ago, some two thousand years or so, there lived a rich man with a good and beautiful wife. They loved each other dearly, but sorrowed much that they had no children. So greatly did they desire to have one, that the wife prayed for it day and night, but still they remained childless.

In front of the house there was a court, in which grew a juniper-tree. One winter's day the wife stood under the tree to peel some apples, and as she was peeling them, she cut her finger, and the blood fell on the snow. "Ah," sighed the woman heavily, "if I had but a child, as red as blood and as white as snow," and as she spoke the words, her heart grew light within her, and it seemed to her that her wish was granted, and she returned to the house feeling glad and comforted. A month passed, and the snow had all disappeared; then another month went by, and all the earth was green. So the months followed one another, and first the trees budded in the woods, and soon the green branches grew thickly intertwined, and then the blossoms began to fall. Once again the wife stood under the juniper-tree, and it was so full of sweet scent that her heart leaped for joy, and she was so overcome with her happiness, that she fell on her knees. Presently the fruit became round and firm, and she was glad and at peace; but when they were fully ripe she picked the berries and ate eagerly of them, and then she grew sad and ill. A little while later she called her husband, and said to him, weeping. "If I die, bury me under the juniper-tree." Then she felt comforted and happy again, and before another month had passed she had a little child, and when she saw that it was as white as snow and as red as blood, her joy was so great that she died.

Her husband buried her under the juniper-tree, and wept bitterly for her. By degrees, however, his sorrow grew less, and although at times he still grieved over his loss, he was able to go about as usual, and later on he married again.

He now had a little daughter born to him; the child of his first wife was a boy, who was as red as blood and as white as snow. The mother loved her daughter very much, and when she looked at her and then looked at the boy, it pierced her heart to think that he would always stand in the way of her own child, and she was continually thinking how she could get the whole of the property for her. This evil thought took possession of her more and more, and made her behave very unkindly to the boy. She drove him from place to place with cuffings and buffetings, so that the poor child went about in fear, and had no peace from the time he left school to the time he went back.

One day the little daughter came running to her mother in the store-room, and said, "Mother, give me an apple." "Yes, my child," said the wife, and she gave her a beautiful apple out of the chest; the chest had a very heavy lid and a large iron lock.

"Mother," said the little daughter again, "may not brother have one too?" The mother was angry at this, but she answered, "Yes, when he comes out of school."

Just then she looked out of the window and saw him coming, and it seemed as if an evil spirit entered into her, for she snatched the apple out of her little daughter's hand, and said, "You shall not have one before your brother." She threw the apple into the chest and shut it to. The little boy now came in, and the evil spirit in the wife made her say kindly to him, "My son, will you have an apple?" but she gave him a wicked look. "Mother," said the boy, "how dreadful you look! Yes, give me an apple." The thought came to her that she would kill him. "Come with me," she said, and she lifted up the lid of the chest; "take one out for yourself." And as he bent over to do so, the evil spirit urged her, and crash! down went the lid, and off went the little boy's head. Then she was overwhelmed with fear at the thought of what she had done. "If only I can prevent anyone knowing that I did it," she thought. So she went upstairs to her room, and took a white handkerchief out of her top drawer; then she set the boy's head again on his shoulders, and bound it with the handkerchief so that nothing could be seen, and placed him on a chair by the door with an apple in his hand.

Soon after this, little Marleen came up to her mother who was stirring a pot of boiling water over the fire, and said, "Mother, brother is sitting by the door with an apple in his hand, and he looks so pale; and when I asked him to give me the apple, he did not answer, and that frightened me."

"Go to him again," said her mother, "and if he does not answer, give him a box on the ear." So little Marleen went, and said, "Brother, give me that apple," but he did not say a word; then she gave him a box on the ear, and his head rolled off. She was so terrified at this, that she ran crying and screaming to her mother. "Oh!" she said, "I have knocked off brother's head," and then she wept and wept, and nothing would stop her.

"What have you done!" said her mother, "but no one must know about it, so you must keep silence; what is done can't be undone; we will make him into puddings." And she took the little boy and cut him up, made him into puddings, and put him in the pot. But Marleen stood looking on, and wept and wept, and her tears fell into the pot, so that there was no need of salt.

Presently the father came home and sat down to his dinner; he asked, "Where is my son?" The mother said nothing, but gave him a large dish of black pudding, and Marleen still wept without ceasing.

The father again asked, "Where is my son?"

"Oh," answered the wife, "he is gone into the country to his mother's great uncle; he is going to stay there some time."

"What has he gone there for, and he never even said goodbye to me!"

"Well, he likes being there, and he told me he should be away quite six weeks; he is well looked after there."

"I feel very unhappy about it," said the husband, "in case it should not be all right, and he ought to have said goodbye to me."

With this he went on with his dinner, and said, "Little Marleen, why do you weep? Brother will soon be back." Then he asked his wife for more pudding, and as he ate, he threw the bones under the table.

Little Marleen went upstairs and took her best silk handkerchief out of her bottom drawer, and in it she wrapped all the bones from under the table and carried them outside, and all the time she did nothing but weep. Then she laid them in the green grass under the juniper-tree, and she had no sooner done so, then all her sadness seemed to leave her, and she wept no more. And now the juniper-tree began to move, and the branches waved backwards and forwards, first away from one another, and then together again, as it might be someone clapping their hands for joy. After this a mist came round the tree, and in the midst of it there was a burning as of fire, and out of the fire there flew a beautiful bird, that rose high into the air, singing magnificently, and when it could no more be seen, the juniper-tree stood there as before, and the silk handkerchief and the bones were gone.

Little Marleen now felt as lighthearted and happy as if her brother were still alive, and she went back to the house and sat down cheerfully to the table and ate.

The bird flew away and alighted on the house of a goldsmith and began to sing:

> *"My mother killed her little son;*
> *My father grieved when I was gone;*
> *My sister loved me best of all;*
> *She laid her kerchief over me,*
> *And took my bones that they might lie*
> *Underneath the juniper-tree*
> *Kywitt, Kywitt, what a beautiful bird am I!"*

The goldsmith was in his workshop making a gold chain, when he heard the song of the bird on his roof. He thought it so beautiful that he got up and ran out, and as he crossed the threshold he lost one of his slippers. But he ran on into the middle of the street, with a slipper on one foot and a sock on the other; he still had on his apron, and still held the gold chain and the pincers in his hands, and so he stood gazing up at the bird, while the sun came shining brightly down on the street.

"Bird," he said, "how beautifully you sing! Sing me that song again."

"Nay," said the bird, "I do not sing twice for nothing. Give that gold chain, and I will sing it you again."

"Here is the chain, take it," said the goldsmith. "Only sing me that again."

The bird flew down and took the gold chain in his right claw, and then he alighted again in front of the goldsmith and sang:

> *"My mother killed her little son;*
> *My father grieved when I was gone;*
> *My sister loved me best of all;*
> *She laid her kerchief over me,*
> *And took my bones that they might lie*
> *Underneath the juniper-tree*
> *Kywitt, Kywitt, what a beautiful bird am I!"*

Then he flew away, and settled on the roof of a shoemaker's house and sang:

> *"My mother killed her little son;*
> *My father grieved when I was gone;*
> *My sister loved me best of all;*
> *She laid her kerchief over me,*
> *And took my bones that they might lie*
> *Underneath the juniper-tree*
> *Kywitt, Kywitt, what a beautiful bird am I!"*

The shoemaker heard him, and he jumped up and ran out in his shirt-sleeves, and stood looking up at the bird on the roof with his hand over his eyes to keep himself from being blinded by the sun.

"Bird," he said, "how beautifully you sing!" Then he called through the door to his wife: "Wife, come out; here is a bird, come and look at it and hear how beautifully it sings." Then he called his daughter and the children, then the apprentices, girls and boys, and they all ran up the street to look at the bird, and saw how splendid it was with its red and green feathers, and its neck like burnished gold, and eyes like two bright stars in its head.

"Bird," said the shoemaker, "sing me that song again."

"Nay," answered the bird, "I do not sing twice for nothing; you must give me something."

"Wife," said the man, "go into the garret; on the upper shelf you will see a pair of red shoes; bring them to me." The wife went in and fetched the shoes.

"There, bird," said the shoemaker, "now sing me that song again."

The bird flew down and took the red shoes in his left claw, and then he went back to the roof and sang:

> *"My mother killed her little son;*
> *My father grieved when I was gone;*

My sister loved me best of all;
She laid her kerchief over me,
And took my bones that they might lie
Underneath the juniper-tree
Kywitt, Kywitt, what a beautiful bird am I!"

When he had finished, he flew away. He had the chain in his right claw and the shoes in his left, and he flew right away to a mill, and the mill went "Click clack, click clack, click clack." Inside the mill were twenty of the miller's men hewing a stone, and as they went "Hick hack, hick hack, hick hack," the mill went "Click clack, click clack, click clack."

The bird settled on a lime-tree in front of the mill and sang:

"My mother killed her little son;

then one of the men left off,

My father grieved when I was gone;

two more men left off and listened,

My sister loved me best of all;

then four more left off,

She laid her kerchief over me,
And took my bones that they might lie

now there were only eight at work,

Underneath

And now only five,

the juniper-tree.

And now only one,

Kywitt, Kywitt, what a beautiful bird am I!"

then he looked up and the last one had left off work.

"Bird," he said, "what a beautiful song that is you sing! Let me hear it too; sing it again."

"Nay," answered the bird, "I do not sing twice for nothing; give me that millstone, and I will sing it again."

"If it belonged to me alone," said the man, "you should have it."

"Yes, yes," said the others: "if he will sing again, he can have it."

The bird came down, and all the twenty millers set to and lifted up the stone with a beam; then the bird put his head through the hole and took the stone round his neck like a collar, and flew back with it to the tree and sang:

> *"My mother killed her little son;*
> *My father grieved when I was gone;*
> *My sister loved me best of all;*
> *She laid her kerchief over me,*
> *And took my bones that they might lie*
> *Underneath the juniper-tree*
> *Kywitt, Kywitt, what a beautiful bird am I!"*

And when he had finished his song, he spread his wings, and with the chain in his right claw, the shoes in his left, and the millstone round his neck, he flew right away to his father's house.

The father, the mother, and little Marleen were having their dinner.

"How lighthearted I feel," said the father, "so pleased and cheerful."

"And I," said the mother, "I feel so uneasy, as if a heavy thunderstorm were coming."

But little Marleen sat and wept and wept.

Then the bird came flying towards the house and settled on the roof.

"I do feel so happy," said the father, "and how beautifully the sun shines; I feel just as if I were going to see an old friend again."

"Ah!" said the wife, "and I am so full of distress and uneasiness that my teeth chatter, and I feel as if there were a fire in my veins," and she tore open her dress; and all the while little Marleen sat in the corner and wept, and the plate on her knees was wet with her tears.

The bird now flew to the juniper-tree and began singing:

"My mother killed her little son;

the mother shut her eyes and her ears, that she might see and hear nothing, but there was a roaring sound in her ears like that of a violent storm, and in her eyes a burning and flashing like lightning:

My father grieved when I was gone;

"Look, mother," said the man, "at the beautiful bird that is singing so magnificently; and how warm and bright the sun is, and what a delicious scent of spice in the air!"

My sister loved me best of all;

then little Marleen laid her head down on her knees and sobbed.

"I must go outside and see the bird nearer," said the man.

"Ah, do not go!" cried the wife. "I feel as if the whole house were in flames!"

But the man went out and looked at the bird.

She laid her kerchief over me,

And took my bones that they might lie
Underneath the juniper-tree
Kywitt, Kywitt, what a beautiful bird am I!"

With that the bird let fall the gold chain, and it fell just round the man's neck, so that it fitted him exactly.

He went inside, and said, "See, what a splendid bird that is; he has given me this beautiful gold chain, and looks so beautiful himself."

But the wife was in such fear and trouble, that she fell on the floor, and her cap fell from her head.

Then the bird began again:

"*My mother killed her little son;*

"Ah me!" cried the wife, "if I were but a thousand feet beneath the earth, that I might not hear that song."

My father grieved when I was gone;

then the woman fell down again as if dead.

My sister loved me best of all;

"Well," said little Marleen, "I will go out too and see if the bird will give me anything."

So she went out.

She laid her kerchief over me,
And took my bones that they might lie

and he threw down the shoes to her,

Underneath the juniper-tree
Kywitt, Kywitt, what a beautiful bird am I!"

And she now felt quite happy and lighthearted; she put on the shoes and danced and jumped about in them. "I was so miserable," she said, "when I came out, but that has all passed away; that is indeed a splendid bird, and he has given me a pair of red shoes."

The wife sprang up, with her hair standing out from her head like flames of fire. "Then I will go out too," she said, "and see if it will lighten my misery, for I feel as if the world were coming to an end."

But as she crossed the threshold, crash! the bird threw the millstone down on her head, and she was crushed to death.

The father and little Marleen heard the sound and ran out, but they only saw mist and flame and fire rising from the spot, and when these had passed, there stood the little brother, and he took the father and little Marleen by the hand; then they all three rejoiced, and went inside together and sat down to their dinners and ate.

THE GOLDEN GOOSE

There was a man who had three sons, the youngest of whom was called Dunderhead, and was despised, mocked, and put down on every occasion.

It happened, that the eldest wanted to go into the forest to hew wood. Before he went his mother gave him a beautiful sweet cake and a bottle of wine, that he might not suffer from hunger or thirst.

When he entered the forest, there met him a little old Gray Man who bade him good-day, and said, "Do give me a piece of cake out of your pocket, and let me have a draught of your wine. I am so hungry and thirsty."

But the prudent youth answered, "If I give you my cake and wine, I shall have none for myself. Be off with you," and he left the Little Man standing and went on.

But when he began to hew down a tree, it was not long before he made a false stroke, and the axe cut him in the arm. So he had to go home and have it bound up. And this was the little Gray Man's doing.

After this, the second son went into the forest, and his mother gave him, like the eldest, a cake and a bottle of wine. The little old Gray Man met him likewise, and asked him for a piece of cake and a drink of wine. But the second son, too, said with much reason, "What I give you will be taken away from myself. Be off!" and he left the Little Man standing and went on.

His punishment, however, was not delayed. When he had made a few strokes at the tree, he struck himself in the leg. So he had to be carried home.

Then Dunderhead said, "Father, do let me go and cut wood."

The father answered, "Your brothers have hurt themselves doing so. Leave it alone. You do not understand anything about it."

But Dunderhead begged so long that at last he said, "Go then. You will get wiser by hurting yourself."

His mother gave him a cake made with water and baked in the cinders, and with it a bottle of sour beer.

When he came to the forest the little old Gray Man met him likewise, and greeting him said, "Give me a piece of your cake and a drink out of your bottle. I am so hungry and thirsty."

Dunderhead answered, "I have only cinder-cake and sour beer. If that pleases you, we will sit down and eat."

So they sat down, and when Dunderhead pulled out his cinder-cake, it was a fine sweet cake, and the sour beer had become good wine.

So they ate and drank, and after that the Little Man said, "Since you have a good heart, and are willing to divide what you have, I will give you good luck. There stands an old tree. Cut it down, and you will find something at the roots."

Then the old man took leave of him.

Dunderhead went and cut down the tree; and when it fell there was a Goose sitting in the roots, with feathers of pure gold. He lifted her up, and taking her with him, went to an inn, where he thought he would stay the night. Now the host had three daughters, who saw the Goose and were curious to know what such a wonderful bird might be. And each wanted one of its feathers.

The eldest thought, "I shall soon find an opportunity of pulling out a feather," and when Dunderhead was gone out, she seized the Goose by the wing. But her finger and hand remained sticking fast to it.

The second came in soon afterward, thinking only of how she might get a feather for herself, but she had scarcely touched her sister than she was held fast.

At last, the third came with the like intent, and the others screamed out, "Keep away! For goodness' sake keep away!"

But she did not understand why she was to keep away. "The others are there," she thought, "I may as well be there too," and ran to them. But as soon as she had touched her sister, she remained sticking fast to her. So they had to spend the night with the Goose.

The next morning, Dunderhead took the Goose under his arm and set out, without troubling himself about the three girls who were hanging on to it. They were obliged to run after him, now left, now right, just as he was inclined to go.

In the middle of the fields, the parson met them, and when he saw the procession he said, "For shame, you good-for-nothing girls! Why are you running across the fields after this young man? Is that seemly?" At the same time he seized the youngest by the hand in order to pull her away. But as soon as he touched her, he likewise stuck fast, and was obliged to run behind. Before long, the sexton came by and saw his master, the parson, running on foot behind three girls. He was astonished at this, and called out, "Hi! your Reverence! Whither away so quickly? Do not forget that we have a christening today!" and running after him he took him by the sleeve, but was also held fast.

While the five were trotting thus one behind the other, two laborers came with their hoes from the fields. The parson called out to them and begged that they would set him and the sexton free. But they had scarcely touched the sexton, when they were held fast. And now there were seven of them running behind Dunderhead and the Goose.

Soon afterward, he came to a city, where a King ruled who had a daughter who was so serious that no one could make her laugh. So he had put forth a decree that whosoever should make her laugh should marry her. When Dunderhead heard this, he went with his Goose and all her train before the King's Daughter.

As soon as she saw the seven people running on and on, one behind the other, she began to laugh very loudly as if she would never leave off. Thereupon Dunderhead asked to have her for his wife, and the wedding was celebrated.

After the King's death, Dunderhead inherited the Kingdom, and lived a long time contentedly with his wife.

LITTLE SNOW-WHITE

Once upon a time, in the middle of winter, when the flakes of snow were falling like feathers from the sky, a Queen sat at a window sewing, and the frame of the window was made of black ebony.

And whilst she was sewing and looking out of the window at the snow, she pricked her finger with the needle, and three drops of blood fell upon the snow. And the red looked pretty upon the white snow, and she thought to herself, "Would that I had a child as white as snow, as red as blood, and as black as the wood of the window-frame."

Soon after that she had a little daughter, who was as white as snow, and as red as blood, and her hair was as black as ebony. She was therefore called little Snow-White. And when the child was born, the Queen died.

After a year had passed the King took to himself another wife. She was a beautiful woman, but proud and haughty, and she could not bear that any one else should surpass her in beauty. She had a wonderful looking-glass, and when she stood in front of it and looked at herself in it, and said:

> "Looking-Glass, Looking-Glass, on the wall,
> Who in this land is the fairest of all?"

the Looking-Glass answered:

"Thou, O Queen, art the fairest of all!"

Then she was satisfied, for she knew that the Looking-Glass spoke the truth.

But little Snow-White was growing up, and grew more and more beautiful. When she was seven years old she was as beautiful as the day, and more beautiful than the Queen herself. And once when the Queen asked her Looking-Glass:

"Looking-Glass, Looking-Glass, on the wall,
Who in this land is the fairest of all?"

it answered:

"Thou art fairer than all who are here, Lady Queen.
But more beautiful still is Snow-White, I ween."

Then the Queen was shocked, and turned yellow and green with envy. From that hour, whenever she looked at little Snow-White, her heart heaved in her breast, she hated the maiden so much.

And envy and pride grew higher and higher in her heart like a weed, so that she had no peace day or night. She called a huntsman, and said, "Take the child away into the forest. I will no longer have her in my sight. Kill her."

The huntsman obeyed, and took her away. But when he had drawn his knife, and was about to pierce little Snow-White's innocent heart, she began to weep, and said, "Ah, dear Huntsman, leave me my life! I will run away into the wild forest, and never come home again."

And as she was so beautiful, the huntsman had pity on her and said, "Run away, then, you poor child." "The wild beasts will soon have devoured you," thought he, and yet it seemed as if a stone had been rolled from his heart since it was no longer needful for him to kill her.

But now, the poor child was all alone in the great forest, and so terrified that she looked at every leaf of every tree, and did not know what to do. Then she began to run, and ran over sharp stones and through thorns, and the wild beasts ran past her, but did her no harm.

She ran as long as her feet would go, until it was almost evening. Then she saw a little cottage and went into it to rest herself. Everything in the cottage was small, but neater and cleaner than can be told. There was a table on which was a white cover, and seven little plates, and on each plate a little spoon. Moreover, there were seven little knives and forks, and seven little mugs. Against the wall stood seven little beds side by side, and covered with snow-white counterpanes.

Little Snow-White was so hungry and thirsty, that she ate some vegetables and bread from each plate and drank a drop of wine out of each mug, for she did not wish to take all from one only. Then, as she was so tired, she laid herself down on one of the little beds, but none of them suited her. One was too long, another too short, but at last she found that the seventh one was right, so she remained in it, said a prayer and went to sleep.

When it was quite dark the owners of the cottage came back. They were seven Dwarfs who dug and delved in the mountains for ore. They lit their seven candles, and, as it was now light within the cottage, they saw that some one had been there, for everything was not in the same order in which they had left it.

The first said, "Who has been sitting on my chair?"
The second, "Who has been eating off my plate?"
The third, "Who has been taking some of my bread?"
The fourth, "Who has been eating my vegetables?"
The fifth, "Who has been using my fork?"
The sixth, "Who has been cutting with my knife?"
The seventh, "Who has been drinking out of my mug?"

Then the first looked round and saw that there was a little hole on his bed, and he said, "Who has been getting into my bed?"

The others came up and each called out, "Somebody has been lying in my bed too."

But the seventh when he looked at his bed saw little Snow-White, who was lying fast asleep therein. And he called the others, who came running up, and they cried out with astonishment, and brought their seven little candles and let the light fall on little Snow-White.

"Oh, oh!" cried they, "what a lovely child!" and they were so glad that they did not wake her up, but let her sleep on in the bed. And the seventh Dwarf slept with his companions, one hour with each, and so got through the night.

The next morning, little Snow-White awoke, and was frightened when she saw the seven Dwarfs. But they were friendly and asked her what her name was.

"My name is little Snow-White," she answered.

"How have you come to our house?" said the Dwarfs.

Then she told them that the wicked Queen had wished to have her killed, but that the huntsman had spared her life, and that she had run for the whole day, until at last she had found their dwelling.

The Dwarfs said, "If you will take care of our house, cook, make the beds, wash, sew, and knit, and if you will keep everything neat and clean, you may stay with us and you shall want for nothing."

"Yes," said little Snow-White, "with all my heart," and she stayed with them.

She kept the house in order for them. In the mornings they went to the mountains and looked for copper and gold, in the evenings they came back, and then their supper had to be ready.

The maiden was alone the whole day, so the good Dwarfs warned her and said, "Beware of the Queen, she will soon know that you are here. Be sure to let no one come in."

But the Queen, believing that little Snow-White was dead,

could not but think that she herself was again the first and most beautiful of all. She went to her Looking-Glass, and said:

> *"Looking-Glass, Looking-Glass, on the wall,*
> *Who in this land is the fairest of all?"*

and the Glass answered:

> *"Oh, Queen, thou art fairest of all I see,*
> *But over the hills, where the Seven Dwarfs dwell,*
> *Little Snow-White is alive and well,*
> *And none is so fair as she."*

Then she was astounded, for she knew that the Looking-Glass never spoke falsely, and she knew that the huntsman had betrayed her, for that little Snow-White was still alive.

And so she thought and thought again how she might kill her, for so long as she herself was not the fairest in the whole land, envy let her have no rest. And when she had at last thought of something to do, she painted her face, and dressed herself like an old pedler-woman, and no one could have known her.

In this disguise she went over the Seven Mountains to the Seven Dwarfs, and knocked at the door and cried, "Pretty things to sell, very cheap, very cheap!"

Little Snow-White looked out at the window, and called, "Good-day, my dear woman, what have you to sell?"

"Good things, pretty things," she answered; "stay-laces of all colors," and she pulled out one which was woven of bright-colored silk.

"I may let the worthy old woman in," thought little Snow-White, and she unbolted the door and bought the pretty laces.

"Child," said the old woman, "what a fright you look. Come, I will lace you properly for once."

Little Snow-White had no suspicion, but stood before her, and let herself be laced with the new laces. But the old woman laced so quickly and laced so tightly that little Snow-White lost her breath and fell down as if dead.

"Now I am the most beautiful," said the Queen to herself, and ran away.

Not long afterward, in the evening, the Seven Dwarfs came home. But how shocked they were when they saw their dear little Snow-White lying on the ground, and that she neither stirred nor moved, and seemed to be dead. They lifted her up, and, as they saw that she was laced too tightly, they cut the laces. Than she began to breathe a little, and after a while came to life again.

When the Dwarfs heard what had happened, they said, "The old pedler-woman was no one else than the wicked Queen. Take care and let no one come in when we are not with you."

But the wicked woman, when she had reached home, went in front of the Glass and asked:

"Looking-Glass, Looking-Glass, on the wall,
Who in this land is the fairest of all?"

and it answered as before:

"Oh, Queen, thou art fairest of all I see,
But over the hills, where the Seven Dwarfs dwell,
Little Snow-White is alive and well,
And none is so fair as she."

When she heard that, all her blood rushed to her heart with fear, for she saw plainly that little Snow-White was again alive. "But now," she said, "I will think of something that shall put an end to you," and by the help of witchcraft, which she understood, she made a poisonous comb.

Then she disguised herself, and took the shape of another old woman. So she went over the Seven Mountains to the Seven Dwarfs, knocked at the door, and cried, "Good things to sell, cheap, cheap!"

Little Snow-White looked out, and said, "Go away. I cannot let any one come in."

"I suppose you may look," said the old woman, and pulled the poisonous comb out and held it up.

It pleased the maiden so well that she let herself be beguiled, and opened the door. When they had made a bargain, the old woman said, "Now I will comb you properly for once."

Poor little Snow-White had no suspicion, and let the Old Woman do as she pleased. But hardly had she put the comb in her hair, then the poison in it took effect, and the maiden fell down senseless.

"You paragon of beauty," said the wicked woman, "you are done for now!" and she went away.

But fortunately it was almost evening, and the Seven Dwarfs came home. When they saw little Snow-White lying as if dead upon the ground, they at once suspected the Queen. They looked and found the poisoned comb. Scarcely had they taken it out, when little Snow-White came to herself, and told them what had happened. Then they warned her once more to be upon her guard, and to open the door to no one.

The Queen, at home, went in front of the Glass and said:

"Looking-Glass, Looking-Glass, on the wall,
Who in this land is the fairest of all?"

then it answered as before:

"Oh, Queen, thou art fairest of all I see,
But over the hills, where the Seven Dwarfs dwell,
Little Snow-White is alive and well,
And none is so fair as she."

When she heard the Glass speak thus, she trembled and shook with rage. "Little Snow-White shall die," she cried, "even if it costs me my life!"

Thereupon she went into a secret, lonely room, where no

one ever came, and there she made a very poisonous apple. Outside it looked pretty, white with a red cheek, so that every one who saw it longed for it. But whoever ate a piece of it must surely die.

When the apple was ready, she painted her face, and dressed herself as a countrywoman, and so she went over the Seven Mountains to the Seven Dwarfs. She knocked at the door. Little Snow-White put her head out of the window and said, "I cannot let any one in. The Seven Dwarfs have forbidden me."

"It is all the same to me," answered the woman, "I shall soon get rid of my apples. There, I will give you one."

"No," said little Snow-White, "I dare not take anything."

"Are you afraid of poison?" said the old woman. "Look, I will cut the apple in two pieces. You eat the red cheek, and I will eat the white."

The apple was so cunningly made that only the red cheek was poisoned. Little Snow-White longed for the fine apple, and when she saw that the woman ate part of it, she could resist no longer, and stretched out her hand and took the poisonous half. But hardly had she a bit of it in her mouth, than she fell down dead.

Then the Queen looked at her with a dreadful look, and laughed aloud, and said, "White as snow, red as blood, black as ebony-wood! This time the Dwarfs cannot wake you up again!"

And when she asked of the Looking-Glass at home:

> "*Looking-Glass, Looking-Glass, on the wall,*
> *Who in this land is the fairest of all?*"

it answered at last:

> "*Oh, Queen, in this land thou art fairest of all.*"

Then her envious heart had rest, so far as an envious heart can have rest.

The Dwarfs, when they came home in the evening, found little Snow-White lying upon the ground. She breathed no longer and was dead. They lifted her up, looked to see whether they could find anything poisonous, unlaced her, combed her hair, washed her with water and wine, but it was all of no use. The poor child was dead, and remained dead. They laid her upon a bier, and all seven of them sat round it and wept for her, and wept three days long.

Then they were going to bury her, but she still looked as if she was living, and still had her pretty red cheeks. They said, "We could not bury her in the dark ground," and they had a transparent coffin of glass made, so that she might be seen from all sides. They laid her in it, and wrote her name upon it in golden letters, and that she was a King's Daughter.

Then they put the coffin out upon the mountain, and one of them always stayed by it to watch it. And birds came too, and wept for little Snow-White; first an owl, then a raven, and last a dove.

And now little Snow-White lay a long, long time in the coffin. She did not change, but looked as if she were asleep; for she was as white as snow, as red as blood, and her hair was as black as ebony.

It happened, however, that a King's Son came into the forest, and went to the Dwarfs' house to spend the night. He saw the coffin on the mountain, and the beautiful little Snow-White within it, and read what was written upon it in golden letters.

Then he said to the Dwarfs, "Let me have the coffin. I will give you whatever you want for it."

But the Dwarfs answered, "We will not part with it for all the gold in the world."

Then he said, "Let me have it as a gift, for I cannot live without seeing little Snow-White. I will honor and prize her as my dearest possession," As he spoke in this way the good Dwarfs took pity upon him, and gave him the coffin.

And now the King's Son had it carried away by his servants

on their shoulders. And it happened, that they stumbled over a tree-stump, and with the shock the poisonous piece of apple, which little Snow-White had bitten off, came out of her throat. And before long she opened her eyes, lifted up the lid of the coffin, sat up, and was once more alive.

"Oh, where am I?" she cried.

The King's Son, full of joy, said, "You are with me," and told her what had happened, and said, "I love you more than everything in the world. Come with me to my father's palace, you shall be my wife."

And little Snow-White was willing, and went with him, and their wedding was held with great show and splendor. But the wicked Queen was also bidden to the feast. When she had arrayed herself in beautiful clothes, she went before the Looking-Glass, and said:

> "Looking-Glass, Looking-Glass, on the wall,
> Who in this land is the fairest of all?"

the Glass answered:

> "Oh, Queen, of all here the fairest art thou,
> But the young Queen is fairer by far, I trow!"

Then the wicked woman uttered a curse, and was so wretched, so utterly wretched, that she knew not what to do. At first she would not go to the wedding at all, but she had no peace, and must go to see the young Queen.

And when she went in she knew little Snow-White. And she stood still with rage and fear, and could not stir. But iron slippers had already been put upon the fire, and they were brought in with tongs, and set before her. Then she was forced to put on the red-hot shoes, and dance until she dropped down dead.

THE SEVEN RAVENS

There was once a man who had seven sons, but never a daughter no matter how much he wished for one.

At length, his wife had a child, and it was a daughter. The joy was great. But the child was sickly and small, and so weak that it had to be baptized at once.

The father sent one of the boys in a hurry to the spring, to fetch water for the baptism. The other six boys ran along with him. And as each strove to be the first to fill the jug, it fell into the spring. There they stood, and did not know what to do. None of them dared to go home.

When they did not come back, the father grew impatient, and said, "They have forgotten all about it in a game of play, the wicked boys!"

Soon he grew afraid lest the child should die without being baptized, and he cried out in anger, "I wish the boys were all turned into Ravens!"

Hardly was the word spoken, before he heard a whirring of wings in the air above his head. He looked up, and saw seven coal-black Ravens flying high and away.

The parents could not recall the curse. And though they grieved over the loss of their seven sons, yet they comforted themselves somewhat with their dear little daughter, who soon grew strong and every day more beautiful.

For a long time, she did not know that she had had brothers. Her parents were careful not to mention them before her. But one day, she chanced to overhear some people talking about her, and saying, "that the maiden is certainly beautiful, but really to blame for the misfortune of her seven brothers."

Then she was much troubled, and went to her father and mother, and asked if it was true that she had had brothers, and what was become of them.

The parents did not dare to keep the secret longer, and said that her birth was only the innocent cause of what had happened to her brothers. But the maiden laid it daily to heart, and thought that she must deliver her brothers.

She had no peace and rest until she set out secretly, and went forth into the wide world to seek them out, and set them free, let it cost what it might. She took nothing with her but a little ring belonging to her parents as a keepsake, a loaf of bread against hunger, a little pitcher of water against thirst, and a little chair as a provision against weariness.

And now, she went continually onward, far, far, to the very end of the world. Then she came to the Sun, but it was too hot and terrible, and devoured little children. Hastily she ran away, and ran to the Moon, but it was far too cold, and also awful and malicious. And when it saw the child, it said:

> "*I smell, I smell*
> *The flesh of men!*"

On this she ran swiftly away, and came to the Stars, which were kind and good to her, and each of them sat on its own little chair. But the Morning Star arose, and gave her the drumstick of a chicken, and said, "If you have not that drumstick you cannot open the Glass Mountain, and in the Glass Mountain are your brothers."

The maiden took the drumstick, wrapped it carefully in

a cloth, and went onward again until she came to the Glass Mountain. The door was shut, and she thought she would take out the drumstick. But when she undid the cloth, it was empty, and she had lost the good Star's present. What was she now to do? She wished to rescue her brothers, and had no key to the Glass Mountain. The good little sister took a knife, cut off one of her little fingers, put it in the door, and succeeded in opening it.

When she had got inside, a little Dwarf came to meet her, who said, "My Child, what are you looking for?"

"I am looking for my brothers, the Seven Ravens," she replied.

The Dwarf said, "The Lord Ravens are not at home, but if you wish to wait here until they come, step in."

Thereupon the little Dwarf carried the Ravens' dinner in, on seven little plates, and in seven little glasses. The little sister ate a morsel from each plate, and from each little glass she took a sip. But in the last little glass she dropped the ring which she had brought away with her.

Suddenly, she heard a whirring of wings and a rushing through the air, and then the little Dwarf said, "Now the Lord Ravens are flying home."

Then they came, and wanted to eat and drink, and looked for their little plates and glasses. Then said one after the other, "Who has eaten something from my plate? Who has drunk out of my little glass? It was a human mouth."

And when the seventh came to the bottom of the glass, the ring rolled against his mouth. Then he looked at it, and saw that it was a ring belonging to his father and mother, and said, "God grant that our little sister may be here, and then we shall be free."

When the maiden, who was standing behind the door watching, heard that wish, she came forth, and on this all the Ravens were restored to their human form again. And they embraced and kissed each other, and went joyfully home.

HANSEL AND GRETEL

Hard by a great forest dwelt a poor wood-cutter with his wife and his two children. The boy was called Hansel and the girl Gretel. He had little to bite and to break, and once when great dearth fell on the land, he could no longer procure even daily bread. Now when he thought over this by night in his bed, and tossed about in his anxiety, he groaned and said to his wife: "What is to become of us? How are we to feed our poor children, when we no longer have anything even for ourselves?" "I'll tell you what, husband," answered the woman, "early tomorrow morning we will take the children out into the forest to where it is the thickest; there we will light a fire for them, and give each of them one more piece of bread, and then we will go to our work and leave them alone. They will not find the way home again, and we shall be rid of them." "No, wife," said the man, "I will not do that; how can I bear to leave my children alone in the forest? – the wild animals would soon come and tear them to pieces." "O, you fool!" said she, "then we must all four die of hunger, you may as well plane the planks for our coffins," and she left him no peace until he consented. "But I feel very sorry for the poor children, all the same," said the man.

The two children had also not been able to sleep for hunger, and had heard what their stepmother had said to their father. Gretel wept bitter tears, and said to Hansel: "Now all is over with us." "Be quiet, Gretel," said Hansel, "do not distress yourself, I will soon find a way to help us." And when the old folks had fallen asleep, he got up, put on his little coat, opened the door below, and crept outside. The moon shone brightly, and the white pebbles which lay in front of the house glittered like real silver pennies. Hansel stooped and stuffed the little pocket of his coat with as many as he could get in. Then he went back and said to Gretel: "Be comforted, dear little sister, and sleep in peace, God will not forsake us," and he lay down again in his bed. When day dawned, but before the sun had risen, the woman came and awoke the two children, saying: "Get up, you sluggards! we are going into the forest to fetch wood." She gave each a little piece of bread, and said: "There is something for your dinner, but do not eat it up before then, for you will get nothing else." Gretel took the bread under her apron, as Hansel had the pebbles in his pocket. Then they all set out together on the way to the forest. When they had walked a short time, Hansel stood still and peeped back at the house, and did so again and again. His father said: "Hansel, what are you looking at there and staying behind for? Pay attention, and do not forget how to use your legs." "Ah, father," said Hansel, "I am looking at my little white cat, which is sitting up on the roof, and wants to say goodbye to me." The wife said: "Fool, that is not your little cat, that is the morning sun which is shining on the chimneys." Hansel, however, had not been looking back at the cat, but had been constantly throwing one of the white pebble-stones out of his pocket on the road.

When they had reached the middle of the forest, the father said: "Now, children, pile up some wood, and I will light a fire that you may not be cold." Hansel and Gretel gathered brushwood together, as high as a little hill. The brushwood was lighted, and when the flames were burning very high, the woman said: "Now, children, lay yourselves down by the fire and rest, we will go into the forest and cut some wood. When we have done, we will come back and fetch you away."

Hansel and Gretel sat by the fire, and when noon came, each ate a little piece of bread, and as they heard the strokes of the wood-axe they believed that their father was near. It was not the axe, however, but a branch which he had fastened to a withered tree which the wind was blowing backwards and forwards. And as they had been sitting such a long time, their eyes closed with fatigue, and they fell fast asleep. When at last they awoke, it was already dark night. Gretel began to cry and said: "How are we to get out of the forest now?" But Hansel comforted her and said: "Just wait a little, until the moon has risen, and then we will soon find the way." And when the full moon had risen, Hansel took his little sister by the hand, and followed the pebbles which shone like newly-coined silver pieces, and showed them the way.

They walked the whole night long, and by break of day came once more to their father's house. They knocked at the door, and when the woman opened it and saw that it was Hansel and Gretel, she said: "You naughty children, why have you slept so long in the forest? – we thought you were never coming back at all!" The father, however, rejoiced, for it had cut him to the heart to leave them behind alone.

Not long afterwards, there was once more great dearth throughout the land, and the children heard their mother saying at night to their father: "Everything is eaten again, we have one half loaf left, and that is the end. The children must go, we will take them farther into the wood, so that they will not find their way out again; there is no other means of saving ourselves!" The man's heart was heavy, and he thought: "It would be better for you to share the last mouthful with your children." The woman, however, would listen to nothing that he had to say, but scolded and reproached him. He who says A must say B, likewise, and as he had yielded the first time, he had to do so a second time also.

The children, however, were still awake and had heard the conversation. When the old folks were asleep, Hansel again got up, and wanted to go out and pick up pebbles as he had done before, but the woman had locked the door, and Hansel could not get out. Nevertheless he comforted his little sister, and said: "Do not cry, Gretel, go to sleep quietly, the good God will help us."

Early in the morning came the woman, and took the children out of their beds. Their piece of bread was given to them, but it was still smaller than the time before. On the way into the forest Hansel crumbled his in his pocket, and often stood still and threw a morsel on the ground. "Hansel, why do you stop and look round?" said the father, "go on." "I am looking back at my little pigeon which is sitting on the roof, and wants to say goodbye to me," answered Hansel. "Fool!" said the woman, "that is not your little pigeon, that is the morning sun that is shining on the chimney." Hansel, however little by little, threw all the crumbs on the path.

The woman led the children still deeper into the forest, where they had never in their lives been before. Then a great fire was again made, and the mother said: "Just sit there, you children, and when you are tired you may sleep a little; we are going into the forest to cut wood, and in the evening when we are done, we will come and fetch you away." When it was noon, Gretel shared her piece of bread with Hansel, who had scattered his by the way. Then they fell asleep and evening passed, but no one came to the poor children. They did not awake until it was dark night, and Hansel comforted his little sister and said: "Just wait, Gretel, until the moon rises, and then we shall see the crumbs of bread which I have strewn about, they will show us our way home again." When the moon came they set out, but they found no crumbs, for the many thousands of birds which fly about in the woods and fields had picked them all up. Hansel said to Gretel: "We shall soon find the way," but they did not find it. They walked the whole night and all the next day too from morning till evening, but they did not get out of the forest, and were very hungry, for they had nothing to eat but two or three berries, which grew on the ground. And as they were so weary that their legs would carry them no longer, they lay down beneath a tree and fell asleep.

It was now three mornings since they had left their father's house. They began to walk again, but they always came deeper into the forest, and if help did not come soon, they must die of hunger and weariness. When it was mid-day, they saw a beautiful snow-white bird sitting on a bough, which sang so delightfully that they stood still and listened to it. And when its song was over, it spread its wings and flew away before them, and they followed it until they reached a little house, on the roof of which it alighted; and when they approached the little house they saw that it was built of bread and covered with cakes, but that the windows were of clear sugar. "We will set to work on that," said Hansel, "and have a good meal. I will eat a bit of the roof, and you Gretel, can eat some of the window, it will taste sweet." Hansel reached up above, and broke off a little of the roof to try how it tasted, and Gretel leant against the window and nibbled at the panes. Then a soft voice cried from the parlour:

> "*Nibble, nibble, gnaw,*
> *Who is nibbling at my little house?*"

The children answered:

> "*The wind, the wind,*
> *The heaven-born wind,*"

and went on eating without disturbing themselves. Hansel, who liked the taste of the roof, tore down a great piece of it, and Gretel pushed out the whole of one round window-pane, sat down, and enjoyed herself with it. Suddenly the door opened, and a woman as old as the hills, who supported herself on crutches, came creeping out. Hansel and Gretel were so terribly frightened that they let fall what they had in their hands. The old woman, however, nodded her head, and said: "Oh, you dear children, who has brought you here? do come in, and stay with me. No harm shall happen to you." She took them both by the hand, and led them into her little house. Then good food was set before them, milk and pancakes, with sugar, apples, and nuts. Afterwards two pretty little beds were covered with clean white linen, and Hansel and Gretel lay down in them, and thought they were in heaven.

The old woman had only pretended to be so kind; she was in reality a wicked witch, who lay in wait for children, and had only built the little house of bread in order to entice them there. When a child fell into her power, she killed it, cooked and ate it, and that was a feast day with her. Witches have red eyes, and cannot see far, but they have a keen scent like the beasts, and are aware when human beings draw near. When Hansel and Gretel came into her neighbourhood, she laughed with malice, and said mockingly: "I have them, they shall not escape me again!" Early in the morning before the children were awake, she was already up, and when she saw both of them sleeping and looking so pretty, with their plump and rosy cheeks she muttered to herself: "That will be a dainty mouthful!" Then she seized Hansel with her shrivelled hand, carried him into a little stable, and locked him in behind a grated door. Scream as he might, it would not help him. Then she went to Gretel, shook her till she awoke, and cried: "Get up, lazy thing, fetch some water, and cook something good for your brother, he is in the stable outside, and is to be made fat. When he is fat, I will eat him." Gretel began to weep bitterly, but it was all in vain, for she was forced to do what the wicked witch commanded.

And now the best food was cooked for poor Hansel, but Gretel got nothing but crab-shells. Every morning the woman crept to the little stable, and cried: "Hansel, stretch out your finger that I may feel if you will soon be fat." Hansel, however, stretched out a little bone to her, and the old woman, who had dim eyes, could not see it, and thought it was Hansel's finger, and was astonished that there was no way of fattening him. When four weeks had gone by, and Hansel still remained thin, she was seized with impatience and would not wait any longer. "Now, then, Gretel," she cried to the girl, "stir yourself, and bring some water. Let Hansel be fat or lean, tomorrow I will kill him, and cook him." Ah, how the poor little sister did lament when she had to fetch the water, and how her tears did flow down her cheeks! "Dear God, do help us," she cried. "If the wild beasts in the forest had but devoured us, we should at any rate have died together." "Just keep your noise to yourself," said the old woman, "it won't help you at all."

Early in the morning, Gretel had to go out and hang up the cauldron with the water, and light the fire. "We will bake first," said the old woman, "I have already heated the oven, and kneaded the dough." She pushed poor Gretel out to the oven, from which flames of fire were already darting. "Creep in," said the witch, "and see if it is properly heated, so that we can put the bread in." And once Gretel was inside, she intended to shut the oven and let her bake in it, and then she would eat her, too. But Gretel saw what she had in mind, and said: "I do not know how I am to do it; how do I get in?" "Silly goose," said the old woman. "The door is big enough; just look, I can get in myself!" and she crept up and thrust her head into the oven. Then Gretel gave her a push that drove her far into it, and shut the iron door, and fastened the bolt. Oh! then she began to howl quite horribly, but Gretel ran away and the godless witch was miserably burnt to death.

Gretel, however, ran like lightning to Hansel, opened his little stable, and cried: "Hansel, we are saved! The old witch is dead!" Then Hansel sprang like a bird from its cage when the door is opened. How they did rejoice and embrace each other, and dance about and kiss each other! And as they had no longer any need to fear her, they went into the witch's house, and in every corner there stood chests full of pearls and jewels. "These are far better than pebbles!" said Hansel, and thrust into his pockets whatever could be got in, and Gretel said: "I, too, will take something home with me," and filled her pinafore full. "But now we must be off," said Hansel, "that we may get out of the witch's forest."

When they had walked for two hours, they came to a great stretch of water. "We cannot cross," said Hansel, "I see no foot-plank, and no bridge." "And there is also no ferry," answered Gretel, "but a white duck is swimming there: if I ask her, she will help us over." Then she cried:

> *"Little duck, little duck, dost thou see,*
> *Hansel and Gretel are waiting for thee?*
> *There's never a plank, or bridge in sight,*
> *Take us across on thy back so white."*

The duck came to them, and Hansel seated himself on its back, and told his sister to sit by him. "No," replied Gretel, "that will be too heavy for the little duck; she shall take us across, one after the other." The good little duck did so, and when they were once safely across and had walked for a short time, the forest seemed to be more and more familiar to them, and at length they saw from afar their father's house. Then they began to run, rushed into the parlour, and threw themselves round their father's neck. The man had not known one happy hour since he had left the children in the forest; the woman, however, was dead. Gretel emptied her pinafore until pearls and precious stones ran about the room, and Hansel threw one handful after another out of his pocket to add to them. Then all anxiety was at an end, and they lived together in perfect happiness. My tale is done, there runs a mouse; whosoever catches it, may make himself a big fur cap out of it.

THE STORY OF THE YOUTH WHO WENT FORTH TO LEARN WHAT FEAR WAS

A certain father had two sons, the elder of whom was smart and sensible, and could do everything, but the younger was stupid and could neither learn nor understand anything, and when people saw him they said: "There's a fellow who will give his father some trouble!" When anything had to be done, it was always the elder who was forced to do it; but if his father bade him fetch anything when it was late, or in the night-time, and the way led through the churchyard, or any other dismal place, he answered: "Oh, no father, I'll not go there, it makes me shudder!" for he was afraid. Or when stories were told by the fire at night which made the flesh creep, the listeners sometimes said: "Oh, it makes us shudder!" The younger sat in a corner and listened with the rest of them, and could not imagine what they could mean. "They are always saying: 'It makes me shudder, it makes me shudder!' It does not make me shudder," thought he. "That, too, must be an art of which I understand nothing!"

Now it came to pass that his father said to him one day: "Hearken to me, you fellow in the corner there, you are growing tall and strong, and you too must learn something by which you can earn your bread. Look how your brother works, but you do not even earn your salt." "Well, father," he replied, "I am quite willing to learn something – indeed, if it could but be managed, I should like to learn how to shudder. I don't understand that at all yet." The elder brother smiled when he heard that, and thought to himself: "Goodness, what a blockhead that brother of mine is! He will never be good for anything as long as he lives! He who wants to be a sickle must bend himself betimes."

The father sighed, and answered him: "You shall soon learn what it is to shudder, but you will not earn your bread by that."

Soon after this the sexton came to the house on a visit, and the father bewailed his trouble, and told him how his younger son was so backward in every respect that he knew nothing and learnt nothing. "Just think," said he, "when I asked him how he was going to earn his bread, he actually wanted to learn to shudder." "If that be all," replied the sexton, "he can learn that with me. Send him to me, and I will soon polish him." The father was glad to do it, for he thought: "It will train the boy a little." The sexton therefore took him into his house, and he had to ring the church bell. After a day or two, the sexton awoke him at midnight, and bade him arise and go up into the church tower and ring the bell. "You shall soon learn what shuddering is," thought he, and secretly went there before him; and when the boy was at the top of the tower and turned round, and was just going to take hold of the bell rope, he saw a white figure standing on the stairs opposite the sounding hole. "Who is there?" cried he, but the figure made no reply, and did not move or stir. "Give an answer," cried the boy, "or take yourself off, you have no business here at night."

The sexton, however, remained standing motionless that the boy might think he was a ghost. The boy cried a second time: "What do you want here? – speak if you are an honest fellow, or I will throw you down the steps!" The sexton thought: "He can't mean to be as bad as his words," uttered no sound and stood as if he were made of stone. Then the boy called to him for the third time, and as that was also to no purpose, he ran against him and pushed the ghost down the stairs, so that it fell down the ten steps and remained lying there in a corner. Thereupon he rang the bell, went home, and without saying a word went to bed, and fell asleep. The sexton's wife waited a long time for her husband, but he did not come back. At length she became uneasy, and wakened the boy, and asked: "Do you know where my husband is? He climbed up the tower before you did." "No, I don't know," replied the boy, "but someone was standing by the sounding hole on the other side of the steps, and as he would neither give an answer nor go away, I took him for a scoundrel, and threw him downstairs. Just go there and you will see if it was he. I should be sorry if it were." The woman ran away and found her husband, who was lying moaning in the corner, and had broken his leg.

She carried him down, and then with loud screams she hastened to the boy's father, "Your boy," cried she, "has been the cause of a great misfortune! He has thrown my husband down the steps so that he broke his leg. Take the good-for-nothing fellow out of our house." The father was terrified, and ran thither and scolded the boy. "What wicked tricks are these?" said he. "The devil must have put them into your head." "Father," he replied, "do listen to me. I am quite innocent. He was standing there by night like one intent on doing evil. I did not know who it was, and I entreated him three times either to speak or to go away." "Ah," said the father, "I have nothing but unhappiness with you. Go out of my sight. I will see you no more."

"Yes, father, right willingly, wait only until it is day. Then will I go forth and learn how to shudder, and then I shall, at any rate, understand one art which will support me." "Learn what you will," spoke the father, "it is all the same to me. Here are fifty talers for you. Take these and go into the wide world, and tell no one from whence you come, and who is your father, for I have reason to be ashamed of you." "Yes, father, it shall be as you will. If you desire nothing more than that, I can easily keep it in mind."

When the day dawned, therefore, the boy put his fifty talers into his pocket, and went forth on the great highway, and continually said to himself: "If I could but shudder! If I could but shudder!" Then a man approached who heard this conversation which the youth was holding with himself, and when they had walked a little farther to where they could see the gallows, the man said to him: "Look, there is the tree where seven men have married the ropemaker's daughter, and are now learning how to fly. Sit down beneath it, and wait till night comes, and you will soon learn how to shudder." "If that is all that is wanted," answered the youth, "it is easily done; but if I learn how to shudder as fast as that, you shall have my fifty talers. Just come back to me early in the morning." Then the youth went to the gallows, sat down beneath it, and waited till evening came. And as he was cold, he lighted himself a fire, but at midnight the wind blew so sharply that in spite of his fire, he could not get warm. And as the wind knocked the hanged men against each other, and they moved backwards and forwards, he thought to himself: "If you shiver below by the fire, how those up above must freeze and suffer!" And as he felt pity for them, he raised the ladder, and climbed up, unbound one of them after the other, and brought down all seven. Then he stoked the fire, blew it, and set them all round it to warm themselves. But they sat there and did not stir, and the fire caught their clothes. So he said: "Take care, or I will hang you up again." The dead men, however, did not hear, but were quite silent, and let their rags go on burning. At this he grew angry, and said: "If you will not take care, I cannot help you, I will not be burnt with you," and he hung them up again each in his turn. Then he sat down by his fire and fell asleep, and the next morning the man came to him and wanted to have the fifty talers, and said: "Well do you know how to shudder?" "No," answered he, "how should I know? Those fellows up there did not open their mouths, and were so stupid that they let the few old rags which they had on their bodies get burnt." Then the man saw that he would not get the fifty talers that day, and went away saying: "Such a youth has never come my way before."

The youth likewise went his way, and once more began to mutter to himself: "Ah, if I could but shudder! Ah, if I could but shudder!" A waggoner who was striding behind him heard this and asked: "Who are you?" "I don't know," answered the youth. Then the waggoner asked: "From whence do you come?" "I know not." "Who is your father?" "That I may not tell you." "What is it that you are always muttering between your teeth?" "Ah," replied the youth, "I do so wish I could shudder, but no one can teach me how." "Enough of your foolish chatter," said the waggoner. "Come, go with me, I will see about a place for you." The youth went with the waggoner, and in the evening they arrived at an inn where they wished to pass the night. Then at the entrance of the parlour the youth again said quite loudly: "If I could but shudder! If I could but shudder!" The host who heard this, laughed and said: "If that is your desire, there ought to be a good opportunity for you here." "Ah, be silent," said the hostess, "so many prying persons have already lost their lives, it would be a pity and a shame if such beautiful eyes as these should never see the daylight again."

But the youth said: "However difficult it may be, I will learn it. For this purpose indeed have I journeyed forth." He let the host have no rest, until the latter told him, that not far from thence stood a haunted castle where anyone could very easily learn what shuddering was, if he would but watch in it for three nights. The king had promised that he who would venture should have his daughter to wife, and she was the most beautiful maiden the sun shone on. Likewise in the castle lay great treasures, which were guarded by evil spirits, and these treasures would then be freed, and would make a poor man rich enough. Already many men had gone into the castle, but as yet none had come out again. Then the youth went next morning to the king, and said: "If it be allowed, I will willingly watch three nights in the haunted castle."

The king looked at him, and as the youth pleased him, he said: "You may ask for three things to take into the castle with you, but they must be things without life." Then he answered: "Then I ask for a fire, a turning lathe, and a cutting-board with the knife."

The king had these things carried into the castle for him during the day. When night was drawing near, the youth went up and made himself a bright fire in one of the rooms, placed the cutting-board and knife beside it, and seated himself by the turning-lathe. "Ah, if I could but shudder!" said he, "but I shall not learn it here either." Towards midnight he was about to poke his fire, and as he was blowing it, something cried suddenly from one corner: "Au, miau! how cold we are!" "You fools!" cried he, "what are you crying about? If you are cold, come and take a seat by the fire and warm yourselves." And when he had said that, two great black cats came with one tremendous leap and sat down on each side of him, and looked savagely at him with their fiery eyes. After a short time, when they had warmed themselves, they said: "Comrade, shall we have a game of cards?" "Why not?" he replied, "but just show me your paws." Then they stretched out their claws. "Oh," said he, "what long nails you have! Wait, I must first cut them for you." Thereupon he seized them by the throats, put them on the cutting-board and screwed their feet fast. "I have looked at your fingers," said he, "and my fancy for card-playing has gone," and he struck them dead and threw them out into the water. But when he had made away with these two, and was about to sit down again by his fire, out from every hole and corner came black cats and black dogs with red-hot chains, and more and more of them came until he could no longer move, and they yelled horribly, and got on his fire, pulled it to pieces, and tried to put it out. He watched them for a while quietly, but at last when they were going too far, he seized his cutting-knife, and cried: "Away with you, vermin," and began to cut them down. Some of them ran away, the others he killed, and threw out into the fish-pond. When he came back he fanned the embers of his fire again and warmed himself. And as he thus sat, his eyes would keep open no longer, and he felt a desire to sleep. Then he looked round and saw a great bed in the corner. "That is the very thing for me," said he, and got into it. When he was just going to shut his eyes, however, the bed began to move of its own accord, and went over the whole of the castle. "That's right," said he, "but go faster." Then the bed rolled on as if six horses were harnessed to it, up and down, over thresholds and stairs, but suddenly hop, hop, it turned over upside down, and lay on him like a mountain. But he threw quilts and pillows up in the air, got out and said: "Now anyone who likes, may drive," and lay down by his fire, and slept till it was day. In the morning the king came, and when he saw him lying there on the ground, he thought the evil spirits had killed him and he was dead. Then said he: "After all it is a pity, – for so handsome a man." The youth heard it, got up, and said: "It has not come to that yet." Then the king was astonished, but very glad, and asked how he had fared. "Very well indeed," answered he; "one night is past, the two others will pass likewise." Then he went to the innkeeper, who opened his eyes very wide, and said: "I never expected to see you alive again! Have you learnt how to shudder yet?" "No," said he, "it is all in vain. If someone would but tell me!"

The second night he again went up into the old castle, sat down by the fire, and once more began his old song: "If I could but shudder!" When midnight came, an uproar and noise of tumbling about was heard; at first it was low, but it grew louder and louder. Then it was quiet for a while, and at length with a loud scream, half a man came down the chimney and fell before him. "Hullo!" cried he, "another half belongs to this. This is not enough!" Then the uproar began again, there was a roaring and howling, and the other half fell down likewise. "Wait," said he, "I will just stoke up the fire a little for you." When he had done that and looked round again, the two pieces were joined together, and a hideous man was sitting in his place. "That is no part of our bargain," said the youth, "the bench is mine." The man wanted to push him away; the youth, however, would not allow that, but thrust him off with all his strength, and seated himself again in his own place. Then still more men fell down, one after the other; they brought nine dead men's legs and two skulls, and set them up and played at nine-pins with them. The youth also wanted to play and said: "Listen you, can I join you?" "Yes, if you have any money." "Money enough," replied he, "but your balls are not quite round." Then he took the skulls and put them in the lathe and turned them till they were round. "There, now they will roll better!" said he. "Hurrah! now we'll have fun!" He played with them and lost some of his money, but when it struck twelve, everything vanished from his sight. He lay down and quietly fell asleep. Next morning the king came to inquire after him. "How has it fared with you this time?" asked he. "I have been playing at nine-pins," he answered, "and have lost a couple of farthings." "Have you not shuddered then?" "What?" said he, "I have had a wonderful time! If I did but know what it was to shudder!"

The third night he sat down again on his bench and said quite sadly: "If I could but shudder." When it grew late, six tall men came in and brought a coffin. Then he said: "Ha, ha, that is certainly my little cousin, who died only a few days ago," and he beckoned with his finger, and cried: "Come, little cousin, come." They placed the coffin on the ground, but he went to it and took the lid off, and a dead man lay therein. He felt his face, but it was cold as ice. "Wait," said he, "I will warm you a little," and went to the fire and warmed his hand

and laid it on the dead man's face, but he remained cold. Then he took him out, and sat down by the fire and laid him on his breast and rubbed his arms that the blood might circulate again. As this also did no good, he thought to himself: "When two people lie in bed together, they warm each other," and carried him to the bed, covered him over and lay down by him. After a short time the dead man became warm too, and began to move. Then said the youth, "See, little cousin, have I not warmed you?" The dead man, however, got up and cried: "Now will I strangle you."

"What!" said he, "is that the way you thank me? You shall at once go into your coffin again," and he took him up, threw him into it, and shut the lid. Then came the six men and carried him away again. "I cannot manage to shudder," said he. "I shall never learn it here as long as I live."

Then a man entered who was taller than all others, and looked terrible. He was old, however, and had a long white beard. "You wretch," cried he, "you shall soon learn what it is to shudder, for you shall die." "Not so fast," replied the youth. "If I am to die, I shall have to have a say in it." "I will soon seize you," said the fiend. "Softly, softly, do not talk so big. I am as strong as you are, and perhaps even stronger." "We shall see," said the old man. "If you are stronger, I will let you go – come, we will try." Then he led him by dark passages to a smith's forge, took an axe, and with one blow struck an anvil into the ground. "I can do better than that," said the youth, and went to the other anvil. The old man placed himself near and wanted to look on, and his white beard hung down. Then the youth seized the axe, split the anvil with one blow, and in it caught the old man's beard. "Now I have you," said the youth. "Now it is your turn to die." Then he seized an iron bar and beat the old man till he moaned and entreated him to stop, when he would give him great riches. The youth drew out the axe and let him go. The old man led him back into the castle, and in a cellar showed him three chests full of gold. "Of these," said he, "one part is for the poor, the other for the king, the third yours." In the meantime it struck twelve, and the spirit disappeared, so that the youth stood in darkness. "I shall still be able to find my way out," said he, and felt about, found the way into the room, and slept there by his fire. Next morning the king came and said: "Now you must have learnt what shuddering is?" "No," he answered; "what can it be? My dead cousin was here, and a bearded man came and showed me a great deal of money down below, but no one told me what it was to shudder." "Then," said the king, "you have saved the castle, and shall marry my daughter." "That is all very well," said he, "but still I do not know what it is to shudder!"

Then the gold was brought up and the wedding celebrated; but howsoever much the young king loved his wife, and however happy he was, he still said always: "If I could but shudder – if I could but shudder." And this at last angered her. Her waiting-maid said: "I will find a cure for him; he shall soon learn what it is to shudder." She went out to the stream which flowed through the garden, and had a whole bucketful of gudgeons brought to her. At night when the young king was sleeping, his wife was to draw the clothes off him and empty the bucket full of cold water with the gudgeons in it over him, so that the little fishes would sprawl about him. Then he woke up and cried: "Oh, what makes me shudder so? – what makes me shudder so, dear wife? Ah! now I know what it is to shudder!"

THE KING OF THE
GOLDEN MOUNTAIN

There was once a merchant who had only one child, a son, that was very young, and barely able to run alone. He had two richly laden ships then making a voyage upon the seas, in which he had embarked all his wealth, in the hope of making great gains, when the news came that both were lost. Thus from being a rich man he became all at once so very poor that nothing was left to him but one small plot of land; and there he often went in an evening to take his walk, and ease his mind of a little of his trouble.

One day, as he was roaming along in a brown study, thinking with no great comfort on what he had been and what he now was, and was like to be, all on a sudden there stood before him a little, rough-looking, black dwarf. "Prithee, friend, why so sorrowful?" said he to the merchant; "what is it you take so deeply to heart?" "If you would do me any good I would willingly tell you," said the merchant. "Who knows but I may?" said the little man: "tell me what ails you, and perhaps you will find I may be of some use." Then the merchant told him how all his wealth was gone to the bottom of the sea, and how he had nothing left but that little plot of land. "Oh, trouble not yourself about that," said the dwarf; "only undertake to bring me here, twelve years hence, whatever meets you first on your going home, and I will give you as much as you please." The merchant thought this was no great thing to ask; that it would most likely be his dog or his cat, or something of that sort, but forgot his little boy Heinel; so he agreed to the bargain, and signed and sealed the bond to do what was asked of him.

But as he drew near home, his little boy was so glad to see him that he crept behind him, and laid fast hold of his legs, and looked up in his face and laughed. Then the father started, trembling with fear and horror, and saw what it was that he had bound himself to do; but as no gold was come, he made himself easy by thinking that it was only a joke that the dwarf was playing him, and that, at any rate, when the money came, he should see the bearer, and would not take it in.

About a month afterwards he went upstairs into a lumber-room to look for some old iron, that he might sell it and raise a little money; and there, instead of his iron, he saw a large pile of gold lying on the floor. At the sight of this he was overjoyed, and forgetting all about his son, went into trade again, and became a richer merchant than before.

Meantime little Heinel grew up, and as the end of the twelve years drew near the merchant began to call to mind his bond, and became very sad and thoughtful; so that care and sorrow were written upon his face. The boy one day asked what was the matter, but his father would not tell for some time; at last, however, he said that he had, without knowing it, sold him for gold to a little, ugly-looking, black dwarf, and that the twelve years were coming round when he must keep his word. Then Heinel said, "Father, give yourself very little trouble about that; I shall be too much for the little man."

When the time came, the father and son went out together to the place agreed upon: and the son drew a circle on the ground, and set himself and his father in the middle of it. The little black dwarf soon came, and walked round and round about the circle, but could not find any way to get into it, and he either could not, or dared not, jump over it. At last the boy said to him. "Have you anything to say to us, my friend, or what do you want?" Now Heinel had found a friend in a good fairy, that was fond of him, and had told him what to do; for this fairy knew what good luck was in store for him. "Have you brought me what you said you would?" said the dwarf to the merchant. The old man held his tongue, but Heinel said again, "What do you want here?" The dwarf said, "I come to talk with your father, not with you." "You have cheated and taken in my father," said the son; "pray give him up his bond at once." "Fair and softly," said the little old man; "right is right; I have paid my money, and your father has had it, and spent it; so be so good as to let me have what I paid it for." "You must have my consent to that first," said Heinel, "so please to step in here, and let us talk it over." The old man grinned, and showed his teeth, as if he should have been very glad to get into the circle if he could. Then at last, after a long talk, they came to terms. Heinel agreed that his father must give him up, and that so far the dwarf should have his way: but, on the other hand, the fairy had told Heinel what fortune was in store for him, if he followed his own course; and he did not choose to be given up to his hump-backed friend, who seemed so anxious for his company.

So, to make a sort of drawn battle of the matter, it was settled that Heinel should be put into an open boat, that lay on the sea-shore hard by; that the father should push him off with his own hand, and that he should thus be set adrift, and left to the bad or good luck of wind and weather. Then he took leave of his father, and set himself in the boat, but before it got far off a wave struck it, and it fell with one side low in the water, so the merchant thought that poor Heinel was lost, and went home very sorrowful, while the dwarf went his way, thinking that at any rate he had had his revenge.

The boat, however, did not sink, for the good fairy took care of her friend, and soon raised the boat up again, and it went safely on. The young man sat safe within, till at length it ran ashore upon an unknown land. As he jumped upon the shore he saw before him a beautiful castle but empty and dreary within, for it was enchanted. "Here," said he to himself, "must I find the prize the good fairy told me of." So he once more searched the whole palace through, till at last he found a white snake, lying coiled up on a cushion in one of the chambers.

Now the white snake was an enchanted princess; and she was very glad to see him, and said, "Are you at last come to set me free? Twelve long years have I waited here for the fairy to bring you hither as she promised, for you alone can save me. This night twelve men will come: their faces will be black, and they will be dressed in chain armour. They will ask what you do here, but give no answer; and let them do what they will – beat, whip, pinch, prick, or torment you – bear all; only speak not a word, and at twelve o'clock they must go away. The second night twelve others will come: and the third night twenty-four, who will even cut off your head; but at the twelfth hour of that night their power is gone, and I shall be free, and will come and bring you the Water of Life, and will wash you with it, and bring you back to life and health." And all came to pass as she had said; Heinel bore all, and spoke not a word; and the third night the princess came, and fell on his neck and kissed him. Joy and gladness burst forth throughout the castle, the wedding was celebrated, and he was crowned king of the Golden Mountain.

They lived together very happily, and the queen had a son. And thus eight years had passed over their heads, when the king thought of his father; and he began to long to see him once again. But the queen was against his going, and said, "I know well that misfortunes will come upon us if you go." However, he gave her no rest till she agreed. At his going away she gave him a wishing-ring, and said, "Take this ring, and put it on your finger; whatever you wish it will bring you; only promise never to make use of it to bring me hence to your father's house." Then he said he would do what she asked, and put the ring on his finger, and wished himself near the town where his father lived.

Heinel found himself at the gates in a moment; but the guards would not let him go in, because he was so strangely clad. So he went up to a neighbouring hill, where a shepherd dwelt, and borrowed his old frock, and thus passed unknown into the town. When he came to his father's house, he said he was his son; but the merchant would not believe him, and said he had had but one son, his poor Heinel, who he knew was long since dead: and as he was only dressed like a poor shepherd, he would not even give him anything to eat. The king, however, still vowed that he was his son, and said, "Is there no mark by which you would know me if I am really your son?" "Yes," said his mother, "our Heinel had a mark like a raspberry on his right arm." Then he showed them the mark, and they knew that what he had said was true.

He next told them how he was king of the Golden Mountain, and was married to a princess, and had a son seven years old. But the merchant said, "that can never be true; he must be a fine king truly who travels about in a shepherd's frock!" At this the son was vexed; and forgetting his word, turned his ring, and wished for his queen and son. In an instant they stood before him; but the queen wept, and said he had broken his word, and bad luck would follow. He did all he could to soothe her, and she at last seemed to be appeased; but she was not so in truth, and was only thinking how she should punish him.

One day he took her to walk with him out of the town, and showed her the spot where the boat was set adrift upon the wide waters. Then he sat himself down, and said, "I am very much tired; sit by me, I will rest my head in your lap, and sleep a while." As soon as he had fallen asleep, however, she drew the ring from his finger, and crept softly away, and wished herself and her son at home in their kingdom. And when he awoke he found himself alone, and saw that the ring was gone from his finger. "I can never go back to my father's house," said he; "they would say I am a sorcerer: I will journey forth into the world, till I come again to my kingdom."

So saying he set out and travelled till he came to a hill, where three giants were sharing their father's goods; and as they saw him pass they cried out and said, "Little men have sharp wits; he shall part the goods between us." Now there was a sword that cut off an enemy's head whenever the wearer gave the words, "Heads off!"; a cloak that made the owner invisible, or gave him any form he pleased; and a pair of boots that carried the wearer wherever he wished. Heinel said they must first let him try these wonderful things, then he might know how to set a value upon them. Then they gave him the cloak, and he wished himself a fly, and in a moment he was a fly. "The cloak is very well," said he: "now give me the sword." "No," said they; "not unless you undertake not to say, 'Heads off!' for if you do we are all dead men." So they gave it him, charging him to try it on a tree. He next asked for the boots also; and the moment he had all three in his power, he wished himself at the Golden Mountain; and there he was at once. So the giants were left behind with no goods to share or quarrel about.

As Heinel came near his castle he heard the sound of merry music; and the people around told him that his queen was about to marry another husband. Then he threw his cloak around him, and passed through the castle hall, and placed himself by the side of the queen, where no one saw him. But when anything to eat was put upon her plate, he took it away and ate it himself; and when a glass of wine was handed to her, he took it and drank it; and thus, though they kept on giving her meat and drink, her plate and cup were always empty.

Upon this, fear and remorse came over her, and she went into her chamber alone, and sat there weeping; and he followed her there. "Alas!" said she to herself, "was I not once set free? Why then does this enchantment still seem to bind me?"

"False and fickle one!" said he. "One indeed came who set thee free, and he is now near thee again; but how have you used him? Ought he to have had such treatment from thee?" Then he went out and sent away the company, and said the wedding was at an end, for that he was come back to the kingdom. But the princes, peers, and great men mocked at him. However, he would enter into no parley with them, but only asked them if they would go in peace or not. Then they turned upon him and tried to seize him; but he drew his sword. "Heads Off!" cried he; and with the word the traitors' heads fell before him, and Heinel was once more king of the Golden Mountain.

JORINDA AND JORINGEL

There was once an old castle in the midst of a large and thick forest, and in it an old woman, who was a Witch, dwelt all alone.

In the daytime, she changed herself into a cat or a screech-owl, but in the evening she took her proper shape again as a human being. She could lure wild beasts and birds to her, then she killed and boiled and roasted them.

If any one came within one hundred paces of the castle he was obliged to stand still, and could not stir from the place until she bade him be free. But whenever an innocent maiden came within this circle, she changed her into a bird, shut her up in a wicker-work cage, and carried the cage into a room in the castle. She had about seven thousand cages of rare birds in the castle.

Now, there was once a maiden who was called Jorinda, who was fairer than all other girls. She and a handsome youth named Joringel had promised to marry each other, and their greatest happiness was being together.

One day, in order that they might be able to talk together in quiet, they went for a walk in the forest.

"Take care," said Joringel, "that you do not go too near the castle."

It was a beautiful evening. The sun shone brightly between the trunks of the trees into the dark green of the forest, and the turtledoves sang mournfully upon the young boughs of the birch-trees.

Jorinda wept now and then. She sat down in the sunshine and was sorrowful. Joringel was sorrowful too. They were as sad as if they were about to die. Then they looked around them, and were quite at a loss, for they did not know by which way to go home. The sun was half above the mountain and half set.

Joringel looked through the bushes, and saw the old walls of the castle close at hand. He was horror-stricken and filled with deadly fear.

Jorinda was singing:

> *"My little Bird, with the necklace red,*
> *Sings sorrow, sorrow, sorrow,*
> *He sings that the Dove must soon be dead,*
> *Sings sorrow, sor——jug, jug, jug!"*

Joringel looked for Jorinda. She was changed into a Nightingale, and sang *"jug, jug, jug!"*

A screech-owl with glowing eyes flew three times round about her, and three times cried, *"to-whoo, to-whoo, to-whoo!"*

Joringel could not move. He stood there like a stone, and could neither weep nor speak, nor move hand or foot.

The sun had now set. The owl flew into the thicket. Directly afterward there came out of it a crooked Old Woman, yellow and lean, with large red eyes and a hooked nose, the point of which reached to her chin. She muttered to herself, caught the Nightingale, and took it away in her hand.

Joringel could neither speak nor move from the spot. The Nightingale was gone.

At last the woman came back, and said in a hollow voice, "Greet thee, Zachiel. If the moon shines on the cage, Zachiel, let him loose at once."

Then Joringel was freed. He fell on his knees before the woman and begged that she would give him back his Jorinda. But she said that he should never have her again, and went away. He called, he wept. He lamented, but all in vain, "Ah, what is to become of me?"

Joringel went away, and at last came to a strange village. There he kept sheep for a long time. He often walked round and round the castle, but not too near to it. One night he dreamt that he found a Blood-Red Flower, in the middle of which was a beautiful large pearl; that he picked the flower and went with it to the castle, and that everything he touched with the flower was freed from enchantment. He also dreamt that by means of it, he recovered his Jorinda.

In the morning, when he awoke, he began to seek over hill and dale to find such a flower. He sought until the ninth day, and then, early in the morning, he found the Blood-Red Flower. In the middle of it, there was a large dew-drop, as big as the finest pearl.

Day and night, he journeyed with this flower to the castle. When he was within a hundred paces of it he was not held fast, but walked on to the door.

Joringel was full of joy. He touched the door with the flower, and it sprang open. He walked in through the courtyard, and listened for the sound of the birds. At last he heard it. He went on, and found the room from whence it came. There the Witch was feeding the birds in the seven thousand cages.

When she saw Joringel, she was angry, very angry, and scolded and spat poison and gall, but she could not come within two paces of him. He did not take any notice of her, but went and looked at the cages with the birds. But there were many hundred Nightingales, how was he to find his Jorinda again?

Just then he saw the Old Woman quietly take away a cage with a bird in it, and go toward the door.

Swiftly he sprang toward her, touched the cage with the flower, and also the Old Woman.

She could now no longer bewitch any one. And Jorinda was standing there, clasping him round the neck, and she was as beautiful as ever!

THE ROBBER BRIDEGROOM

There was once a miller who had one beautiful daughter, and as she was grown up, he was anxious that she should be well married and provided for. He said to himself, "I will give her to the first suitable man who comes and asks for her hand." Not long after a suitor appeared, and as he appeared to be very rich and the miller could see nothing in him with which to find fault, he betrothed his daughter to him. But the girl did not care for the man as a girl ought to care for her betrothed husband. She did not feel that she could trust him, and she could not look at him nor think of him without an inward shudder. One day he said to her, "You have not yet paid me a visit, although we have been betrothed for some time." "I do not know where your house is," she answered. "My house is out there in the dark forest," he said. She tried to excuse herself by saying that she would not be able to find the way thither. Her betrothed only replied, "You must come and see me next Sunday; I have already invited guests for that day, and that you may not mistake the way, I will strew ashes along the path."

When Sunday came, and it was time for the girl to start, a feeling of dread came over her which she could not explain, and that she might be able to find her path again, she filled her pockets with peas and lentils to sprinkle on the ground as she went along. On reaching the entrance to the forest she found the path strewed with ashes, and these she followed, throwing down some peas on either side of her at every step she took. She walked the whole day until she came to the deepest, darkest part of the forest. There she saw a lonely house, looking so grim and mysterious, that it did not please her at all. She stepped inside, but not a soul was to be seen, and a great silence reigned throughout. Suddenly a voice cried:

"Turn back, turn back, young maiden fair,
Linger not in this murderers' lair."

The girl looked up and saw that the voice came from a bird hanging in a cage on the wall. Again it cried:

"Turn back, turn back, young maiden fair,
Linger not in this murderers' lair."

The girl passed on, going from room to room of the house, but they were all empty, and still she saw no one. At last she came to the cellar, and there sat a very, very old woman, who could not keep her head from shaking. "Can you tell me," asked the girl, "if my betrothed husband lives here?"

"Ah, you poor child," answered the old woman, "what a place for you to come to! This is a murderers' den. You think yourself a promised bride, and that your marriage will soon take place, but it is with death that you will keep your marriage feast. Look, do you see that large cauldron of water which I am obliged to keep on the fire! As soon as they have you in their power they will kill you without mercy, and cook and eat you, for they are eaters of men. If I did not take pity on you and save you, you would be lost."

Thereupon the old woman led her behind a large cask, which quite hid her from view. "Keep as still as a mouse," she said; "do not move or speak, or it will be all over with you. Tonight, when the robbers are all asleep, we will flee together. I have long been waiting for an opportunity to escape."

The words were hardly out of her mouth when the godless crew returned, dragging another young girl along with them. They were all drunk, and paid no heed to her cries and lamentations. They gave her wine to drink, three glasses full, one of white wine, one of red, and one of yellow, and with that her heart gave way and she died. Then they tore off her dainty clothing, laid her on a table, and cut her beautiful body into pieces, and sprinkled salt upon it.

The poor betrothed girl crouched trembling and shuddering behind the cask, for she saw what a terrible fate had been intended for her by the robbers. One of them now noticed a gold ring still remaining on the little finger of the murdered girl, and as he could not draw it off easily, he took a hatchet and cut off the finger; but the finger sprang into the air, and fell behind the cask into the lap of the girl who was hiding there. The robber took a light and began looking for it, but he could not find it. "Have you looked behind the large cask?" said one of the others. But the old woman called out, "Come and eat your suppers, and let the thing be till tomorrow; the finger won't run away."

"The old woman is right," said the robbers, and they ceased looking for the finger and sat down.

The old woman then mixed a sleeping draught with their wine, and before long they were all lying on the floor of the cellar, fast asleep and snoring. As soon as the girl was assured of this, she came from behind the cask. She was obliged to step over the bodies of the sleepers, who were lying close together, and every moment she was filled with renewed dread lest she should awaken them. But God helped her, so that she passed safely over them, and then she and the old woman went upstairs, opened the door, and hastened as fast as they could from the murderers' den. They found the ashes scattered by the wind, but the peas and lentils had sprouted, and grown sufficiently above the ground, to guide them in the moonlight along the path. All night long they walked, and it was morning before they reached the mill. Then the girl told her father all that had happened.

The day came that had been fixed for the marriage. The bridegroom arrived and also a large company of guests, for the miller had taken care to invite all his friends and relations. As they sat at the feast, each guest in turn was asked to tell a tale; the bride sat still and did not say a word.

"And you, my love," said the bridegroom, turning to her, "is there no tale you know? Tell us something."

"I will tell you a dream, then," said the bride. "I went alone through a forest and came at last to a house; not a soul could I find within, but a bird that was hanging in a cage on the wall cried:

> *"Turn back, turn back, young maiden fair,*
> *Linger not in this murderers' lair."*

and again a second time it said these words."

"My darling, this is only a dream."

"I went on through the house from room to room, but they were all empty, and everything was so grim and mysterious. At last I went down to the cellar, and there sat a very, very old woman, who could not keep her head still. I asked her if my betrothed lived here, and she answered, 'Ah, you poor child, you are come to a murderers' den; your betrothed does indeed live here, but he will kill you without mercy and afterwards cook and eat you.'"

"My darling, this is only a dream."

"The old woman hid me behind a large cask, and scarcely had she done this when the robbers returned home, dragging a young girl along with them. They gave her three kinds of wine to drink, white, red, and yellow, and with that she died."

"My darling, this is only a dream."

"Then they tore off her dainty clothing, and cut her beautiful body into pieces and sprinkled salt upon it."

"My darling, this is only a dream."

"And one of the robbers saw that there was a gold ring still left on her finger, and as it was difficult to draw off, he took a hatchet and cut off her finger; but the finger sprang into the air and fell behind the great cask into my lap. And here is the finger with the ring." And with these words the bride drew forth the finger and shewed it to the assembled guests.

The bridegroom, who during this recital had grown deadly pale, up and tried to escape, but the guests seized him and held him fast. They delivered him up to justice, and he and all his murderous band were condemned to death for their wicked deeds.

THE ELVES AND THE SHOEMAKER

A shoemaker, by no fault of his own, had become so poor that at last he had nothing left but leather for one pair of shoes. So in the evening, he cut out the shoes which he wished to make the next morning. And as he had a good conscience, he lay down quietly in his bed, commended himself to God, and fell asleep.

In the morning, after he had said his prayers, and was just going to sit down to work, lo! both shoes stood all finished on his table. He was astounded, and did not know what to say. He took the shoes in his hands to examine them closer, and they were so neatly made that there was not one bad stitch in them, just as if they were meant for a masterpiece.

Soon after, a buyer came in, and as the shoes pleased him well, he paid more for them than was customary. And, with the money, the shoemaker was able to purchase leather for two pairs of shoes.

He cut them out at night, and next morning was about to set to work with fresh courage; but he had no need to do so, for, when he got up, they were already made. And buyers also were not wanting, who gave him money enough to buy leather for four pairs of shoes.

The following morning, too, he found the four pairs made. And so it went on constantly, what he cut out in the evening was finished by morning, so that he soon had his honest living again, and at last became a wealthy man.

Now it befell that, one evening not long before Christmas, when the man had been cutting out, he said to his wife, before going to bed, "What think you, if we were to stay up to-night to see who it is that lends us this helping hand?"

The woman liked the idea, and lighted a candle, and then they hid themselves in a corner of the room, behind some clothes which were hanging there, and watched.

When it was midnight, two pretty tiny naked Little Men came, sat down by the shoemaker's table, took all the work which was cut out before them and began to stitch, sew, and hammer so skilfully and so quickly with their little fingers, that the shoemaker could not turn away his eyes for astonishment. They did not stop until all was done, and stood finished on the table, and then they ran quickly away.

Next morning, the woman said, "The Little Men have made us rich, and we really must show that we are grateful for it. They run about so much, and have nothing on, and must be cold. I'll tell you what I'll do. I will make them little shirts, coats, vests, and trousers, and knit both of them a pair of stockings. Do you make them two little pairs of shoes."

The man said, "I shall be very glad to do it."

And one night, when everything was ready, they laid their presents, instead of the cut-out work, all together on the table, and then concealed themselves to see how the Little Men would behave.

At midnight they came bounding in, and wanted to get to work at once. But as they did not find any leather cut out, only the pretty little articles of clothing, they were at first astonished, and then they showed intense delight. They dressed themselves with the greatest rapidity, putting the pretty clothes on, and singing:

"Now we are boys so fine to see,
Why should we longer cobblers be?"

Then they danced and skipped and leapt over chairs and benches. At last, they danced out of doors. From that time forth they came no more, but as long as the shoemaker lived all went well with him, and all his undertakings prospered.

THE WOLF AND THE SEVEN LITTLE KIDS

There was once on a time, an old Goat who had seven little Kids, and loved them with all the love of a mother for her children.

One day, she wanted to go into the forest and fetch some food. So she called all seven to her and said, "Dear Children, I have to go into the forest. Be on your guard against the Wolf. If he come in, he will devour you all – skin, hair, and all. The wretch often disguises himself; but you will know him at once by his rough voice and his black feet."

The Kids said, "Dear Mother, we will take good care of ourselves. You may go away without any anxiety."

Then the old one bleated, and went on her way with an easy mind.

It was not long before some one knocked at the house-door, and cried, "Open the door, dear Children! Your mother is here, and has brought something back with her for each of you."

But the little Kids knew that it was the Wolf, by his rough voice. "We will not open the door," cried they; "you are not our mother. She has a soft, pleasant voice, but your voice is rough. You are the Wolf!"

Then the Wolf went away to a shopkeeper, and bought a great lump of chalk, ate this and made his voice soft with it. Then he came back, knocked at the door of the house, and cried, "Open the door, dear Children! Your mother is here and has brought something back with her for each of you."

But the Wolf had laid his black paws against the window, and the children saw them, and cried, "We will not open the door, our mother has not black feet like you. You are the Wolf!"

Then the Wolf ran to a baker, and said, "I have hurt my feet, rub some dough over them for me."

And when the baker had rubbed his feet over, he ran to the miller and said, "Strew some white meal over my feet for me." The miller thought to himself, "The Wolf wants to deceive some one," and refused. But the Wolf said, "If you will not do it, I will devour you." Then the miller was afraid, and made his paws white for him. Yes! so are men!

Now, the wretch went for the third time to the house-door, knocked at it, and said, "Open the door for me, Children! Your dear little mother has come home, and has brought every one of you something from the forest with her."

The little Kids cried, "First show us your paws that we may know if you are our dear little mother."

Then he put his paws in through the window. And when the Kids saw that they were white, they believed all that he said, and opened the door. But who should come in but *the Wolf*!

They were terrified and wanted to hide themselves. One sprang under the table, the second into the bed, the third into the stove, the fourth into the kitchen, the fifth into the cupboard, the sixth under the washing-bowl, and the seventh into the clock-case. But the Wolf found them all and made no delay, but swallowed one after the other down his throat. The youngest in the clock-case was the only one he did not find.

When the Wolf had satisfied his appetite, he took himself

off, laid himself down under a tree in the green meadow outside, and began to sleep.

Soon afterward, the old Goat came home again from the forest. Ah! what a sight she saw there! The house-door stood wide open. The table, chairs, and benches were thrown down, the washing-bowl lay broken to pieces, and the quilts and pillows were pulled off the bed.

She sought her children, but they were nowhere to be found. She called them one after another by name, but no one answered. At last, when she called the youngest, a soft voice cried, "Dear Mother, I am in the clock-case."

She took the Kid out, and it told her that the Wolf had come and had eaten all the others. Then you may imagine how she wept over her poor children!

At length, in her grief she went out, and the youngest Kid ran with her. When they came to the meadow, there lay the Wolf by the tree and he was snoring so loud that the branches shook. She looked at him on every side and saw that something was moving and struggling in his stomach. "Ah!" said she, "is it possible that my poor children, whom he has swallowed down for his supper, can be still alive?"

Then the Kid had to run home and fetch scissors, and a needle and thread, and the Goat cut open the monster's stomach. Hardly had she made one cut, than a little Kid thrust its head out, and when she had cut farther, all six sprang out one after another, and were all still alive, and had suffered no hurt whatever, for in his greediness the monster had swallowed them whole.

What rejoicing there was! They embraced their dear mother, and jumped like a tailor at his wedding. The mother, however, said, "Now go and look for some big stones. We will fill the wicked beast's stomach with them, while he is asleep."

Then the seven Kids dragged the stones thither with all speed, and put as many of them into his stomach as they could get in. And the mother sewed him up again in the greatest haste; so that he was not aware of anything and never once stirred.

When the Wolf had had his sleep out, he got on his legs, and as the stones in his stomach made him very thirsty, he wanted to go to a well to drink. But when he began to walk and to move about, the stones in his stomach knocked against each other and rattled. Then cried he:

> *"What rumbles and tumbles*
> *Against my poor bones?*
> *I thought 'twas six Kids,*
> *But it's only big stones!"*

And when he got to the well and stooped over the water and was just about to drink, the heavy stones made him fall in. There was no help for it, but he had to drown miserably!

When the seven Kids saw that, they came running to the spot and cried aloud, "The Wolf is dead! The Wolf is dead!" and danced for joy round about the well with their mother.

THE GOLDEN BIRD

In the olden time, there was a King, who had behind his palace a beautiful pleasure-garden, in which there was a tree that bore Golden Apples. When the apples were getting ripe they were counted, but on the very next morning one was missing. This was told to the King, and he ordered that a watch should be kept every night beneath the tree.

The King had three sons, the eldest of whom he sent, as soon as night came, into the garden. But when it was midnight, he could not keep himself from sleeping, and next morning again an apple was gone.

The following night, the second son had to keep watch, it fared no better with him. As soon as twelve o'clock had struck he fell asleep, and in the morning an apple was gone.

Now, it came to the turn of the third son to watch. He was quite ready, but the King had not much trust in him, and thought that he would be of less use than his brothers. But at last he let him go.

The youth lay down beneath the tree, but kept awake, and did not let sleep master him. When it struck twelve, something rustled through the air, and in the moonlight he saw a bird coming whose feathers were shining with gold. The bird alighted on the tree, and had just plucked off an apple, when the youth shot an arrow at him. The bird flew off, but the arrow had struck his plumage, and one of his golden feathers fell down.

The youth picked it up, and the next morning took it to the King and told him what he had seen in the night. The King called his council together, and every one declared that a feather like this was worth more than the whole kingdom.

"If the feather is so precious," declared the King, "one alone will not do for me. I must and will have the whole bird!"

The eldest son set out. He trusted to his cleverness, and thought that he would easily find the Golden Bird. When he had gone some distance he saw a Fox sitting at the edge of a wood, so he cocked his gun and took aim at him.

The Fox cried, "Do not shoot me! And in return I will give you some good counsel. You are on the way to the Golden Bird. This evening you will come to a village in which stand two inns opposite to one another. One of them is lighted up brightly, and all goes on merrily within, but do not enter it. Go rather into the other, even though it seems a bad one."

"How can such a silly beast give wise advice?" thought the King's Son, and he pulled the trigger. But he missed the Fox, who stretched out his tail and ran quickly into the wood.

So he pursued his way, and by evening came to the village where the two inns were. In one they were singing and dancing. The other had a poor, miserable look.

"I should be a fool, indeed," he thought, "if I were to go into the shabby tavern, and pass by the good one." So he went into the cheerful one, lived there in riot and revel, and forgot the bird and his father, and all good counsels.

Some time had passed, and when the eldest son, month after month, did not come home, the second set out, wishing to find the Golden Bird. The Fox met him as he had met the eldest, and gave him the good advice, of which he took no heed. He came to the two inns. His brother was standing at the window of the one from which came the music, and called to him. He could not resist, but went inside, and lived only for pleasure.

Again some time passed, and then the youngest King's Son wanted to set off and try his luck. But his father would not allow it. "It is of no use," said he, "he will be less likely to find the Golden Bird than his brothers. And if a mishap were to befall him, he knows not how to help himself. He is a little wanting at the best." But at last, as he had no peace, he let him go.

Again the Fox was sitting outside the wood, and begged for his life, and offered his good advice. The youth was good-natured, and said, "Be easy, little Fox, I will do you no harm."

"You shall not repent it," answered the Fox; "and that you may proceed more quickly, get up behind on my tail."

And scarcely had he seated himself, when the Fox began to run, and away he went over stock and stone till his hair whistled in the wind. When they came to the village, the youth got off. He followed the good advice, and without looking round turned into the little inn, where he spent the night quietly.

The next morning, as soon as he got into the open country, there sat the Fox already, and said, "I will tell you further what you have to do. Go straight forward. At last you will come to a castle, in front of which a whole regiment of soldiers is lying, but do not trouble yourself about them, for they will all be asleep and snoring.

"Go through the midst of them straight into the castle. Go through all the rooms, till at last you will come to a chamber where a Golden Bird is hanging in a wooden cage. Close by, there stands an empty gold cage for show. Beware of taking the bird out of the common cage and putting it into the fine one, or it may go badly with you."

With these words the Fox again stretched out his tail, and the King's Son seated himself upon it. Away he went over stock and stone, till his hair whistled in the wind.

When he came to the castle he found everything as the Fox had said. The King's Son went into the chamber where the

Golden Bird was shut up in a wooden cage, whilst a golden one stood hard by; and the three Golden Apples lay about the room.

"But," thought he, "it would be absurd if I were to leave the beautiful bird in the common and ugly cage," so he opened the door, laid hold of it, and put it into the golden cage. But at the same moment the bird uttered a shrill cry.

The soldiers awoke, rushed in, and took him off to prison. The next morning he was taken before a court of justice, and as he confessed everything, was sentenced to death.

The King, however, said that he would grant him his life on one condition – namely, if he brought him the Golden Horse which ran faster than the wind. And in that case he should receive, over and above, as a reward, the Golden Bird.

The King's Son set off, but he sighed and was sorrowful, for how was he to find the Golden Horse? But all at once he saw his old friend the Fox sitting on the road.

"Look you," said the Fox, "this has happened because you did not give heed to me. However, be of good courage. I will help you, and tell you how to get to the Golden Horse. You must go straight on, and you will come to a castle, where in the stable stands the horse. The grooms will be lying in front of the stable.

"They will be asleep and snoring, and you can quietly lead out the Golden Horse. But of one thing you must take heed. Put on him the common saddle of wood and leather, and not the golden one, which hangs close by, else it will go ill with you."

Then the Fox stretched out his tail, the King's Son seated himself upon it. Away he went over stock and stone, until his hair whistled in the wind.

Everything happened just as the Fox had said. The King's Son came to the stable in which the Golden Horse was standing, but just as he was going to put the common saddle upon him, he thought, "It will be a shame to such a beautiful beast, if I do not give him the good saddle which belongs to him by right."

But scarcely had the golden saddle touched the horse than he began to neigh loudly. The grooms awoke, seized the youth, and threw him into prison. The next morning he was sentenced by the court to death; but the King promised to grant him his life, and the Golden Horse as well, if he would rescue the beautiful Princess from the Golden Castle.

With a heavy heart the youth set out. Yet luckily for him he soon found the trusty Fox.

"I ought to leave you to your ill-luck," said the Fox, "but I pity you, and will help you once more out of your trouble. This road takes you straight to the Golden Castle. You will reach it by eventide. And at night, when everything is quiet, the beautiful Princess goes to the bathing-house to bathe. When she enters it, run up to her and give her a kiss. Then she will follow you, and you can take her away with you. Only do not allow her to say farewell to her parents first, or it will go ill with you."

Then the Fox stretched out his tail, the King's Son seated himself upon it. Away the Fox went, over stock and stone, till his hair whistled in the wind.

When he reached the Golden Castle it was just as the Fox had said. He waited until midnight, when everything lay in deep sleep, and the beautiful Princess was going to the bathing-house. Then he sprang out and gave her a kiss. She said that she would like to go with him, but she asked him pitifully, and with tears, to be allowed to take leave of her parents.

At first he withstood her prayer, but when she wept more and more, and fell at his feet, he at last gave in. But no sooner had the maiden reached the bedside of her father, than he and all the rest in the castle awoke, and the youth was laid hold of and put into prison.

The next morning, the King said to him, "Your life is forfeited, and you can only find mercy if you take away the hill which stands in front of my windows, and prevents my seeing beyond it. And you must finish it all within eight days. If you do that you shall have my daughter as your reward."

The King's Son began, and dug and shovelled without leaving off. But after seven days when he saw how little he had done, and how all his work was as good as nothing, he fell into great sorrow and gave up all hope.

On the evening of the seventh day the Fox appeared and said, "You do not deserve that I should take any trouble about you. Nevertheless, go away and lie down to sleep. I will do the work for you."

The next morning, when he awoke and looked out of the window, the hill had gone. Full of joy, the youth ran to the King, and told him that the task was fulfilled. And whether he liked it or not, the King had to hold to his word and give him his daughter.

So the two set forth together, and it was not long before the trusty Fox came up with them. "You have certainly got what is best," said he, "but the Golden Horse also belongs to the maiden of the Golden Castle."

"How shall I get it?" asked the youth.

"That I will tell you," answered the Fox; "first take the beautiful maiden to the King who sent you to the Golden Castle. There will be unheard-of rejoicing. They will gladly give you the Golden Horse, and will bring it out to you."

All was brought to pass successfully, and the King's Son carried off the beautiful Princess on the Golden Horse.

The Fox did not remain behind, and he said to the youth, "Now I will help you to get the Golden Bird. When you come near to the castle where the Golden Bird is to be found, let the maiden get down, and I will take her into my care. Then ride with the Golden Horse into the castle yard. There will be great rejoicing at the sight, and they will bring out the Golden Bird for you."

When all was accomplished and the King's Son was about to ride home with his treasures, the Fox said, "Now you shall reward me for my help."

"What do you require for it?" asked the youth.

"When you get into the wood yonder, shoot me dead, and chop off my head and feet."

"That would be fine gratitude," said the King's Son, "I cannot possibly do that for you."

The Fox said, "If you will not do it I must leave you. But before I go away I will give you a piece of good advice. Be careful about two things. Buy no gallows'-flesh, and do not sit at the edge of any well." And then he ran into the wood.

The youth thought, "That is a wonderful beast, he has strange whims. Who is going to buy gallows'-flesh? and the desire to sit at the edge of a well has never yet seized me."

He rode on with the beautiful maiden, and his road took him again through the village in which his two brothers had remained. There was a great stir and noise, and, when he asked what was going on, he was told that two men were going to be hanged. As he came nearer to the place he saw that they were his brothers, who had been playing all kinds of wicked pranks, and had squandered their entire wealth. He inquired whether they could not be set free.

"If you will pay for them," answered the people; "but why should you waste your money on wicked men, and buy them free?"

He did not think twice about it, but paid for them. And when they were set free they all went on their way together.

They came to the wood where the Fox had first met them, and, as it was cool and pleasant within it, whilst the sun shone hotly, the two brothers said, "Let us rest a little by the well, and eat and drink."

He agreed, and whilst they were talking he forgot himself, and sat down upon the edge of the well without foreboding any evil. But the two brothers threw him backwards into the well, took the maiden, the Horse, and the Bird, and went home to their father. "Here we bring you not only the Golden Bird," said they; "we have won the Golden Horse also, and the maiden from the Golden Castle."

Then was there great joy. But the Horse would not eat, the Bird would not sing, and the maiden sat and wept.

But the youngest brother was not dead. By good fortune the well was dry, and he fell upon soft moss without being hurt. But he could not get out again. Even in this strait, the faithful Fox did not leave him. He came and leapt down to him, and upbraided him for having forgotten his advice. "But yet I cannot give it up so," he said; "I will help you up again into daylight." He bade him grasp his tail and keep tight hold of it; and then he pulled him up.

"You are not out of all danger yet," said the Fox. "Your brothers were not sure of your death, and have surrounded the wood with watchers, who are to kill you if you let yourself be seen."

But a poor man was sitting upon the road, with whom the youth changed clothes, and in this way he got to the King's palace.

No one knew him, but the Bird began to sing, the Horse began to eat, and the beautiful maiden left off weeping. The King, astonished, asked, "What does this mean?"

Then the maiden said, "I do not know, but I have been so sorrowful and now I am so happy! I feel as if my true Bridegroom had come." She told him all that had happened, although the other brothers had threatened her with death if she were to betray anything.

The King commanded that all people, who were in his castle, should be brought before him; and amongst them came the youth in his ragged clothes. But the maiden knew him at once and fell upon his neck. The wicked brothers were seized and put to death, but he was married to the beautiful maiden and declared heir to the King.

But how did it fare with the poor Fox? Long afterward, the King's Son was once again walking in the wood, when the Fox met him and said, "You have everything now that you can wish for. But there is never an end to my misery, and yet it is in your power to free me," and again he asked him with tears to shoot him dead and to chop off his head and feet.

So he did it, and scarcely was it done when the Fox was changed into a man, and was no other than the brother of the beautiful Princess, who at last was freed from the magic charm which had been laid upon him.

And now nothing more was wanting to their happiness as long as they lived.

THE VALIANT
LITTLE TAILOR

One summer's morning a little tailor was sitting on his table by the window; he was in good spirits, and sewed with all his might. Then came a peasant woman down the street crying: "Good jams, cheap! Good jams, cheap!" This rang pleasantly in the tailor's ears; he stretched his delicate head out of the window, and called: "Come up here, dear woman; here you will get rid of your goods." The woman came up the three steps to the tailor with her heavy basket, and he made her unpack all the pots for him. He inspected each one, lifted it up, put his nose to it, and at length said: "The jam seems to me to be good, so weigh me out four ounces, dear woman, and if it is a quarter of a pound that is of no consequence." The woman who had hoped to find a good sale, gave him what he desired, but went away quite angry and grumbling. "Now, this jam shall be blessed by God," cried the little tailor, "and give me health and strength"; so he brought the bread out of the cupboard, cut himself a piece right across the loaf and spread the jam over it. "This won't taste bitter," said he, "but

I will just finish the jacket before I take a bite." He laid the bread near him, sewed on, and in his joy, made bigger and bigger stitches. In the meantime the smell of the sweet jam rose to where the flies were sitting in great numbers, and they were attracted and descended on it in hosts. "Hi! who invited you?" said the little tailor, and drove the unbidden guests away. The flies, however, who understood no German, would not be turned away, but came back again in ever-increasing companies. The little tailor at last lost all patience, and drew a piece of cloth from the hole under his work-table, and saying: "Wait, and I will give it to you," struck it mercilessly on them. When he drew it away and counted, there lay before him no fewer than seven, dead and with legs stretched out. "Are you a fellow of that sort?" said he, and could not help admiring his own bravery. "The whole town shall know of this!" And the little tailor hastened to cut himself a girdle, stitched it, and embroidered on it in large letters: "Seven at one stroke!" "What, the town!" he continued, "the whole world shall hear of it!" and his heart wagged with joy like a lamb's tail. The tailor put on the girdle, and resolved to go forth into the world, because he thought his workshop was too small for his valour. Before he went away, he sought about in the house to see if there was anything which he could take with him; however, he found nothing but an old cheese, and that he put in his pocket. In front of the door he observed a bird which had caught itself in the thicket. It had to go into his pocket with the cheese. Now he took to the road boldly, and as he was light and nimble, he felt no fatigue. The road led him up a mountain, and when he had reached the highest point of it, there sat a powerful giant looking peacefully about him. The little tailor went bravely up, spoke to him, and said: "Good day, comrade, so you are sitting there overlooking the wide-spread world! I am just on my way thither, and want to try my luck. Have you any inclination to go with me?" The giant looked contemptuously at the tailor, and said: "You ragamuffin! You miserable creature!"

"Oh, indeed?" answered the little tailor, and unbuttoned

his coat, and showed the giant the girdle, "there may you read what kind of a man I am!" The giant read: "Seven at one stroke," and thought that they had been men whom the tailor had killed, and began to feel a little respect for the tiny fellow. Nevertheless, he wished to try him first, and took a stone in his hand and squeezed it together so that water dropped out of it. "Do that likewise," said the giant, "if you have strength." "Is that all?" said the tailor, "that is child's play with us!" and put his hand into his pocket, brought out the soft cheese, and pressed it until the liquid ran out of it. "Faith," said he, "that was a little better, wasn't it?" The giant did not know what to say, and could not believe it of the little man. Then the giant picked up a stone and threw it so high that the eye could scarcely follow it. "Now, little mite of a man, do that likewise," "Well thrown," said the tailor, "but after all the stone came down to earth again; I will throw you one which shall never come back at all," and he put his hand into his pocket, took out the bird, and threw it into the air. The bird, delighted with its liberty, rose, flew away and did not come back. "How does that shot please you, comrade?" asked the tailor. "You can certainly throw," said the giant, "but now we will see if you are able to carry anything properly." He took the little tailor to a mighty oak tree which lay there felled on the ground, and said: "If you are strong enough, help me to carry the tree out of the forest." "Readily," answered the little man; "take you the trunk on your shoulders, and I will raise up the branches and twigs; after all, they are the heaviest." The giant took the trunk on his shoulder, but the tailor seated himself on a branch, and the giant, who could not look round, had to carry away the whole tree, and the little tailor into the bargain: he behind, was quite merry and happy, and whistled the song: "Three tailors rode forth from the gate," as if carrying the tree were child's play. The giant, after he had dragged the heavy burden part of the way, could go no further, and cried: "Hark you, I shall have to let the tree fall!" The tailor sprang nimbly down, seized the tree with both arms as if he had been carrying it, and said to the giant: "You are such a great fellow, and yet cannot even carry the tree!"

They went on together, and as they passed a cherry-tree, the giant laid hold of the top of the tree where the ripest fruit was hanging, bent it down, gave it into the tailor's hand, and bade him eat. But the little tailor was much too weak to hold the tree, and when the giant let it go, it sprang back again, and the tailor was tossed into the air with it. When he had fallen down again without injury, the giant said: "What is this? Have you not strength enough to hold the weak twig?" "There is no lack of strength," answered the little tailor. "Do you think that could be anything to a man who has struck down seven at one blow? I leapt over the tree because the huntsmen are shooting down there in the thicket. Jump as I did, if you can do it." The giant made the attempt but he could not get over the tree, and remained hanging in the branches, so that in this also the tailor kept the upper hand.

The giant said: "If you are such a valiant fellow, come with me into our cavern and spend the night with us." The little tailor was willing, and followed him. When they went into the cave, other giants were sitting there by the fire, and each of them had a roasted sheep in his hand and was eating it. The little tailor looked round and thought: "It is much more spacious here than in my workshop." The giant showed him a bed, and said he was to lie down in it and sleep. The bed, however, was too big for the little tailor; he did not lie down in it, but crept into a corner. When it was midnight, and the giant thought that the little tailor was lying in a sound sleep, he got up, took a great iron bar, cut through the bed with one blow, and thought he had finished off the grasshopper for good. With the earliest dawn the giants went into the forest, and had quite forgotten the little tailor, when all at once he walked up to them quite merrily and boldly. The giants were terrified, they were afraid that he would strike them all dead, and ran away in a great hurry.

The little tailor went onwards, always following his own

pointed nose. After he had walked for a long time, he came to the courtyard of a royal palace, and as he felt weary, he lay down on the grass and fell asleep. Whilst he lay there, the people came and inspected him on all sides, and read on his girdle: "Seven at one stroke." "Ah!" said they, "what does the great warrior want here in the midst of peace? He must be a mighty lord." They went and announced him to the king, and gave it as their opinion that if war should break out, this would be a weighty and useful man who ought on no account to be allowed to depart. The counsel pleased the king, and he sent one of his courtiers to the little tailor to offer him military service when he awoke. The ambassador remained standing by the sleeper, waited until he stretched his limbs and opened his eyes, and then conveyed to him this proposal. "For this very reason have I come here," the tailor replied, "I am ready to enter the king's service." He was therefore honourably received, and a special dwelling was assigned him.

The soldiers, however, were set against the little tailor, and wished him a thousand miles away. "What is to be the end of this?" they said among themselves. "If we quarrel with him, and he strikes about him, seven of us will fall at every blow; not one of us can stand against him." They came therefore to a decision, betook themselves in a body to the king, and begged for their dismissal. "We are not prepared," said they, "to stay with a man who kills seven at one stroke." The king was sorry that for the sake of one he should lose all his faithful servants, wished that he had never set eyes on the tailor, and would willingly have been rid of him again. But he did not venture to give him his dismissal, for he dreaded lest he should strike him and all his people dead, and place himself on the royal throne. He thought about it for a long time, and at last found good counsel. He sent to the little tailor and caused him to be informed that as he was a great warrior, he had one request to make to him. In a forest of his country lived two giants, who caused great mischief with their robbing, murdering, ravaging, and burning, and no one could approach them without putting himself in danger of death. If the tailor conquered and killed these two giants, he would give him his only daughter to wife, and half of his kingdom as a dowry, likewise one hundred horsemen should go with him to assist him. "That would indeed be a fine thing for a man like me!" thought the little tailor. "One is not offered a beautiful princess and half a kingdom every day of one's life!" "Oh, yes," he replied, "I will soon subdue the giants, and do not require the help of the hundred horsemen to do it; he who can hit seven with one blow has no need to be afraid of two."

The little tailor went forth, and the hundred horsemen followed him. When he came to the outskirts of the forest, he said to his followers: "Just stay waiting here, I alone will soon finish off the giants." Then he bounded into the forest and looked about right and left. After a while he perceived both giants. They lay sleeping under a tree, and snored so that the branches waved up and down. The little tailor, not idle, gathered two pocketsful of stones, and with these climbed up the tree. When he was halfway up, he slipped down by a branch, until he sat just above the sleepers, and then let one stone after another fall on the breast of one of the giants. For a long time the giant felt nothing, but at last he awoke, pushed his comrade, and said: "Why are you knocking me?" "You must be dreaming," said the other, "I am not knocking you." They laid themselves down to sleep again, and then the tailor threw a stone down on the second. "What is the meaning of this?" cried the other "Why are you pelting me?" "I am not pelting you," answered the first, growling. They disputed about it for a time, but as they were weary they let the matter rest, and their eyes closed once more. The little tailor began his game again, picked out the biggest stone, and threw it with all his might on the breast of the first giant. "That is too bad!" cried he, and sprang up like a madman, and pushed his companion against the tree until it shook. The other paid him back in the same coin, and they got into such a rage that they tore up trees and belaboured each other so long, that at last they both fell down dead on the ground at the same time. Then the little tailor leapt down. "It is a lucky thing," said he, "that they did not tear up the tree on which I was sitting, or I should have had to sprint on to another like a squirrel; but we tailors are nimble." He drew out his sword and gave each of them a couple of thrusts in the breast, and then went out to the horsemen and said: "The work is done; I have finished both of them off, but it was hard work! They tore up trees in their sore need, and defended themselves with them, but all that is to no purpose when a man like myself comes, who can kill seven at one blow." "But are you not wounded?" asked the horsemen. "You need not concern yourself about that," answered the tailor, "they have not bent one hair of mine." The horsemen would not believe him, and rode into the forest; there they found the giants swimming in their blood, and all round about lay the torn-up trees.

The little tailor demanded of the king the promised reward; he, however, repented of his promise, and again bethought himself how he could get rid of the hero. "Before you receive my daughter, and the half of my kingdom," said he to him, "you must perform one more heroic deed. In the forest roams a unicorn which does great harm, and you must catch it first." "I fear one unicorn still less than two giants. Seven at one blow, is my kind of affair." He took a rope and an axe with him, went forth into the forest, and again bade those who were sent with him to wait outside. He had not long to seek. The unicorn soon came towards him, and rushed directly on the tailor, as if it would gore him with its horn without more ado. "Softly, softly; it can't be done as quickly as that," said he, and stood still and waited until the animal was quite close, and then sprang nimbly behind the tree. The unicorn ran against the tree with all its strength, and stuck its horn so fast in the trunk that it had not the strength enough to draw it out again, and thus it was caught. "Now, I have got the bird," said the tailor, and came out from behind the tree and put the rope round its neck, and then with his axe he hewed the horn out of the tree, and when all was ready he led the beast away and took it to the king.

The king still would not give him the promised reward, and made a third demand. Before the wedding the tailor was to catch him a wild boar that made great havoc in the forest, and the huntsmen should give him their help. "Willingly," said the tailor, "that is child's play!" He did not take the huntsmen with him into the forest, and they were well pleased that he did not, for the wild boar had several times received them in such a manner that they had no inclination to lie in wait for him. When the boar perceived the tailor, it ran on him with foaming mouth and whetted tusks, and was about to throw him to the ground, but the hero fled and sprang into a chapel which was near and up to the window at once, and in one bound out again. The boar ran after him, but the tailor ran round outside and shut the door behind it, and then the raging beast, which was much too heavy and awkward to leap out of the window, was caught. The little tailor called the huntsmen thither that they might see the prisoner with their own eyes. The hero, however, went to the king, who was now, whether he liked it or not, obliged to keep his promise, and gave his daughter and the half of his kingdom. Had he known that it was no warlike hero, but a little tailor who was standing before him, it would have gone to his heart still more than it did. The wedding was held with great magnificence and small joy, and out of a tailor a king was made.

After some time the young queen heard her husband say in his dreams at night: "Boy, make me the doublet, and patch the pantaloons, or else I will rap the yard-measure over your ears." Then she discovered in what state of life the young lord had been born, and next morning complained of her wrongs to her father, and begged him to help her to get rid of her husband, who was nothing else but a tailor. The king comforted her and said: "Leave your bedroom door open this night, and my servants shall stand outside, and when he has fallen asleep shall go in, bind him, and take him on board a ship which shall carry him into the wide world." The woman was satisfied with this; but the king's armour-bearer, who had heard all, was friendly with the young lord, and informed him of the whole plot. "I'll put a screw into that business," said the little tailor. At night he went to bed with his wife at the usual time, and when she thought that he had fallen asleep, she got up, opened the door, and then lay down again. The little tailor, who was only pretending to be asleep, began to cry out in a clear voice: "Boy, make me the doublet and patch me the pantaloons, or I will rap the yard-measure over your ears. I smote seven at one blow. I killed two giants, I brought away one unicorn, and caught a wild boar, and am I to fear those who are standing outside the room." When these men heard the tailor speaking thus, they were overcome by a great dread, and ran as if the wild huntsman were behind them, and none of them would venture anything further against him. So the little tailor was and remained a king to the end of his life.

CLEVER ELSIE

There was once a man who had a daughter who was called Clever Elsie. And when she had grown up her father said, "We will get her married."

"Yes," said the mother, "if only any one would come who would have her."

At length a man came from a distance, and wooed her, who was called Hans. But he made one condition, that Clever Elsie should be really wise.

"Oh," said the father, "she's sharp enough."

And the mother said, "Oh, she can see the wind coming up the street, and hear the flies coughing."

"Well," said Hans, "if she is not really wise, I won't have her."

When they were sitting at dinner, and had eaten, the mother said, "Elsie, go into the cellar and fetch some beer."

Then Clever Elsie took the pitcher from the wall, went into the cellar, and tapped the lid briskly as she went that the time might not appear long. When she was below she fetched herself a chair, and set it before the barrel, so that she had no need to stoop, and did not hurt her back or do herself any unexpected injury.

Then she placed the can before her, and turned the tap, and while the beer was running, she would not let her eyes be idle, but looked up at the wall. And after much peering here and there, saw a pickaxe exactly above her, which the masons had left there by mistake.

Then Clever Elsie began to weep and said, "If I get Hans, and we have a child, and he grows big, and we send him into the cellar here to draw beer, then the pickaxe will fall on his head and kill him." Then she sat and wept and screamed with all the strength of her body, over the misfortune which lay before her.

Those upstairs waited for the drink, but Clever Elsie still did not come. Then the woman said to the servant, "Just go down into the cellar and see where Elsie is."

The maid went and found her sitting in front of the barrel, screaming loudly.

"Elsie, why do you weep?" asked the maid.

"Ah," she answered, "have I not reason to weep? If I get Hans, and we have a child, and he grows big, and has to draw beer here, the pickaxe may fall on his head, and kill him."

Then said the maid, "What a clever Elsie we have!" and sat down beside her and began loudly to weep over the misfortune.

After a while, as the maid did not come back, and those upstairs were thirsty for the beer, the man said to the boy, "Just go down into the cellar and see where Elsie and the girl are."

The boy went down, and there sat Clever Elsie and the girl both weeping together. Then he asked, "Why are you weeping?"

"Ah," said Elsie, "have I not reason to weep? If I get Hans, and we have a child, and he grows big, and has to draw beer here, the pickaxe will fall on his head and kill him."

Then said the boy, "What a clever Elsie we have!" and sat down by her, and likewise began to howl loudly.

Upstairs they waited for the boy, but as he did not return, the man said to the woman, "Just go down into the cellar and see where Elsie is!"

The woman went down, and found all three in the midst of their lamentations, and inquired what was the cause. Then Elsie told her also, that her future child was to be killed by the pickaxe, when it grew big and had to draw beer, and the pickaxe fell down.

Then said the mother likewise, "What a clever Elsie we have!" and sat down and wept with them.

The man upstairs waited a short time, but as his wife did not come back and his thirst grew ever greater, he said, "I must go into the cellar myself and see where Elsie is."

But when he got into the cellar, and they were all sitting together crying, and he heard the reason, and that Elsie's child was the cause, and that Elsie might perhaps bring one into the world some day, and that it might be killed by the pickaxe, if it should happen to be sitting beneath it, drawing beer just at the very time when it fell, he cried, "Oh, what a clever Elsie!" and sat down, and likewise wept with them.

The Bridegroom stayed up-stairs alone for a long time; then as no one came back he thought, "They must be waiting for me below. I, too, must go there and see what they are about."

When he got down, all five of them were sitting screaming and lamenting quite piteously, each outdoing the other.

"What misfortune has happened then?" asked he.

"Ah, dear Hans," said Elsie, "if we marry each other and have a child, and he is big, and we perhaps send him here to draw something to drink, then the pickaxe which has been left up there might dash his brains out, if it were to fall down, so have we not reason to weep?"

"Come," said Hans, "more understanding than that is not needed for my household, as you are such a clever Elsie, I will have you," and he seized her hand, took her upstairs with him, and married her.

After Hans had had her some time, he said, "Wife, I am going out to work and earn money for us. Go into the field and cut the corn, that we may have some bread."

"Yes, dear Hans, I will do that."

After Hans had gone away, she cooked herself some good broth, and took it into the field with her. When she came to the field she said to herself, "What shall I do? Shall I shear first, or shall I eat first? Oh, I will eat first."

Then she emptied her basin of broth, and when she was fully satisfied, she once more said, "What shall I do? Shall I shear first, or shall I sleep first? I will sleep first." Then she lay down among the corn and fell asleep.

Hans had been at home for a long time, but Elsie did not come. Then said he, "What a clever Elsie I have. She is so industrious, that she does not even come home to eat."

As, however, she still stayed away, and it was evening, Hans went out to see what she had cut. But nothing was cut, and she was lying among the corn, asleep. Then Hans hastened home and brought a fowler's net with little bells and hung it round about her, and she still went on sleeping. Then he ran home, shut the house-door, and sat down in his chair and worked.

At length, when it was quite dark, Clever Elsie awoke and when she got up there was a jingling all round about her, and the bells rang at each step which she took. Then she was frightened, and became uncertain whether she really was Clever Elsie or not, and said, "Is it I, or is it not I?"

But she knew not what answer to make to this, and stood for a time in doubt. At length she thought, "I will go home and ask if it be I, or if it be not I. They will be sure to know."

She ran to the door of her own house, but it was shut. Then she knocked at the window and cried, "Hans, is Elsie within?"

"Yes," answered Hans, "she is within."

Hereupon she was terrified, and said, "Ah, heavens! Then it is not I," and went to another door.

But when the people heard the jingling of the bells, they would not open it, and she could get in nowhere. Then she ran out of the village, and no one has seen her since.

LITTLE BROTHER
AND LITTLE SISTER

Little brother took his little sister by the hand and said, "Since our mother died, we have had no happiness; our stepmother beats us every day, and if we come near her, she kicks us away with her foot. Our meals are the hard crusts of bread that are left over. The little dog under the table is better off, for she often throws it a nice bit. May Heaven pity us! If our mother only knew! Come, we will go forth together into the wide world."

They walked the whole day over meadows, fields, and stony places; and when it rained the little sister said, "Heaven and our hearts are weeping together."

In the evening they came to a large forest, and they were so weary with sorrow and hunger and the long walk, that they lay down in a hollow tree and fell asleep.

The next day when they awoke, the sun was already high and shone down hot into the tree. Then the little brother said, "Little Sister, I am thirsty. If I knew of a little brook I would go and take a drink. I think I hear one running." The little brother got up and took the little sister by the hand, and they set off to find the brook.

But the wicked stepmother was a Witch, and had seen how the two children had gone away. She had crept after them, as Witches do creep, and had bewitched all the brooks in the forest.

Now, when they found a little brook leaping brightly over the stones, the little brother was going to drink out of it, but the little sister heard how it said as it ran:

> *"Who drinks of me, a Tiger be!*
> *Who drinks of me, a Tiger be!"*

Then the little sister cried, "Pray, dear little Brother, do not drink, or you will become a wild beast, and tear me to pieces."

The little brother did not drink, although he was so thirsty, but said, "I will wait for the next spring."

When they came to the next brook, the little sister heard this say:

> *"Who drinks of me, a wild Wolf be!*
> *Who drinks of me, a wild Wolf be!"*

Then the little sister cried out, "Pray, dear little Brother, do not drink, or you will become a Wolf, and devour me."

The little brother did not drink, and said, "I will wait until we come to the next spring, but then I must drink, say what you like; for my thirst is too great."

And when they came to the third brook, the little sister heard how it said as it ran:

> *"Who drinks of me, a Roebuck be!*
> *Who drinks of me, a Roebuck be!"*

The little sister said, "Oh, I pray you, dear little Brother, do not drink, or you will become a Roe, and run away from me."

But the little brother had knelt by the brook, and had bent

down and drunk some of the water. And as soon as the first drops touched his lips, he lay there a young Roe.

And now the little sister wept over her poor bewitched little brother, and the little Roe wept also, and sat sorrowfully near to her. But at last the girl said, "Be quiet, dear little Roe, I will never, never leave you."

Then she untied her golden garter and put it round the Roe's neck, and she plucked rushes and wove them into a soft cord. With this she tied the little animal and led it on; and she walked deeper and deeper into the forest.

And when they had gone a very long way, they came to a little house. The girl looked in; and as it was empty, she thought, "We can stay here and live."

Then she sought for leaves and moss to make a soft bed for the Roe. Every morning she went out and gathered roots and berries and nuts for herself, and brought tender grass for the Roe, who ate out of her hand, and was content and played round about her. In the evening, when the little sister was tired, and had said her prayer, she laid her head upon the Roe's back: that was her pillow, and she slept softly on it. And if only the little brother had had his human form, it would have been a delightful life.

For some time, they were alone like this in the wilderness. But it happened that the King of the country held a great hunt in the forest. Then the blasts of the horns, the barking of dogs, and the merry shouts of the huntsmen rang through the trees, and the Roe heard all, and was only too anxious to be there.

"Oh," said he to his little sister, "let me be off to the hunt, I cannot bear it any longer;" and he begged so much that at last she agreed.

"But," said she to him, "come back to me in the evening. I must shut my door for fear of the rough huntsmen, so knock and say, 'My little Sister, let me in!' that I may know you. And if you do not say that, I shall not open the door."

Then the young Roe sprang away; so happy was he and so merry in the open air.

The King and the huntsmen saw the pretty creature, and started after him. But they could not catch him, and when they thought that they surely had him, away he sprang through the bushes and was gone.

When it was dark he ran to the cottage, knocked, and said, "My little Sister, let me in." Then the door was opened for him, and he jumped in, and rested himself the whole night through upon his soft bed.

The next day, the hunt went on afresh, and when the Roe again heard the bugle-horn, and the *ho! ho!* of the huntsmen, he had no peace, but said, "Sister, let me out, I must be off."

His sister opened the door for him, and said, "But you must be here again in the evening and say your password."

When the King and his huntsmen again saw the young Roe with the golden collar, they all chased him, but he was too quick and nimble for them. This went on for the whole day, but by evening the huntsmen had surrounded him, and one of them wounded him a little in the foot, so that he limped and ran slowly. Then a hunter crept after him to the cottage and heard how he said, "My little Sister, let me in," and saw that the door was opened for him, and was shut again at once.

The huntsman took notice of it all, and went to the King and told him what he had seen and heard. Then the King said, "Tomorrow we will hunt once more."

The little sister, however, was dreadfully frightened when she saw that her little Roe was hurt. She washed the blood off him, laid herbs on the wound, and said, "Go to your bed, dear Roe, that you may get well again."

But the wound was so slight that the Roe, next morning, did not feel it any more. And when he again heard the sport outside, he said, "I cannot bear it, I must be there. They shall not find it so easy to catch me!"

The little sister cried, and said, "This time they will kill you, and here am I alone in the forest, and forsaken by all the world. I will not let you out."

"Then you will have me die of grief," answered the Roe.

"When I hear the bugle-horns I feel as if I must jump out of my skin."

Then the little sister could not do otherwise, but opened the door for him with a heavy heart, and the Roe, full of health and joy, bounded away into the forest.

When the King saw him, he said to his huntsman, "Now chase him all day long till nightfall, but take care that no one does him any harm."

As soon as the sun had set, the King said to the huntsmen, "Now come and show me the cottage in the wood;" and when he was at the door, he knocked and called out, "Dear little Sister, let me in."

Then the door opened, and the King walked in, and there stood a maiden more lovely than any he had ever seen. The maiden was frightened when she saw, not her little Roe, but a man with a golden crown upon his head. But the King looked kindly at her, stretched out his hand, and said:

"Will you go with me to my palace and be my dear wife?"

"Yes, indeed," answered the maiden, "but the little Roe must go with me. I cannot leave him."

The King said, "He shall stay with you as long as you live, and shall want nothing."

Just then he came running in, and the little sister again tied him with the cord of rushes, took it in her own hand, and went away with the King from the cottage.

The King took the lovely maiden upon his horse and carried her to his palace, where the wedding was held with great pomp. She was now the Queen, and they lived for a long time happily together. The Roe was tended and cherished, and ran about in the palace-garden.

But the wicked Witch, because of whom the children had gone out into the world, thought all the time that the little sister had been torn to pieces by the wild beasts in the wood, and that the little brother had been shot for a Roe by the huntsmen. Now when she heard that they were so happy, and so well off, envy and hatred rose in her heart and left her no peace, and she thought of nothing but how she could bring them again to misfortune.

Her own daughter, who was as ugly as night, and had only one eye, grumbled at her and said, "A Queen! that ought to have been my luck."

"Only be quiet," answered the old woman, and comforted her by saying, "when the time comes I shall be ready."

As time went on, the Queen had a pretty little boy. It happened that the King was out hunting; so the old Witch took the form of the chambermaid, went into the room where the Queen lay, and said to her, "Come, the bath is ready. It will do you good, and give you fresh strength. Make haste before it gets cold."

The daughter also was close by; so they carried the weak Queen into the bathroom, and put her into the bath. Then they shut the door and ran away. But in the bathroom they had made a fire of such deadly heat, that the beautiful young Queen was soon suffocated.

When this was done, the old woman took her daughter, put a nightcap on her head, and laid her in bed in place of the Queen. She gave her too the shape and the look of the Queen, only she could not make good the lost eye. But, in order that the King might not see it, she was to lie on the side on which she had no eye.

In the evening, when he came home and heard that he had a son, he was heartily glad, and was going to the bed of his dear wife to see how she was. But the old woman quickly called out, "For your life leave the curtains closed. The Queen ought not to see the light yet, and must have rest."

The King went away, and did not find out that a false Queen was lying in the bed.

But at midnight, when all slept, the nurse, who was sitting in the nursery by the cradle, and who was the only person awake, saw the door open and the true Queen walk in. She took the child out of the cradle, laid it on her arm and nursed it. Then she shook up its pillow, laid the child down again, and covered it with the little quilt. And she did not forget the Roe, but went into the corner where he lay, and stroked his back. Then she went quite silently out of the door again.

The next morning, the nurse asked the guards whether any one had come into the palace during the night, but they answered, "No, we have seen no one."

She came thus many nights and never spoke a word. The nurse always saw her, but she did not dare to tell any one about it.

When some time had passed in this manner, the Queen began to speak in the night, and said:

"How fares my child, how fares my Roe?
Twice shall I come, then never moe!"

The nurse did not answer, but when the Queen had gone again, went to the King and told him all.

The King said, "Ah, heavens! what is this? Tomorrow night I will watch by the child."

In the evening he went into the nursery, and at midnight the Queen again appeared, and said:

"How fares my child, how fares my Roe?
Once shall I come, then never moe!"

And she nursed the child as she was wont to do before she disappeared. The King dared not speak to her, but on the next night he watched again. Then she said:

"How fares my child, How fares my Roe?
This time I come, then never moe!"

At that the King could not restrain himself. He sprang toward her, and said, "You can be none other than my dear wife."

She answered, "Yes, I am your dear wife," and at the same

moment she received life again, and by God's grace became fresh, rosy, and full of health.

Then she told the King the evil deed which the wicked Witch and her daughter had been guilty of toward her. The King ordered both to be led before the judge, and judgment was delivered against them. The daughter was taken into the forest where she was torn to pieces by wild beasts, but the Witch was cast into the fire and miserably burnt.

And as soon as she was burnt the Roe changed his shape, and received his human form again. So the little sister and little brother lived happily together all their lives.

THE BLUE LIGHT

There was once on a time, a soldier who for many years had served the King faithfully. But when the war came to an end he could serve no longer because of the many wounds which he had received.

The King said to him, "You may return to your home, I need you no longer. You will not receive any more money, for only he receives wages who renders me service for them."

Then the soldier did not know how to earn a living, went away greatly troubled, and walked the whole day, until in the evening he entered a forest. When darkness came on, he saw a light, which he went toward, and came to a house wherein lived a Witch.

"Do give me one night's lodging, and a little to eat and drink," said he to her, "or I shall starve."

"Oho!" she answered, "who gives anything to a runaway soldier? Yet will I be compassionate, and take you in, if you will do what I wish."

"What do you wish?" said the soldier.

"That you should dig all round my garden for me, tomorrow."

The soldier consented, and next day labored with all his strength, but could not finish it by the evening.

"I see well enough," said the Witch, "that you can do no more today. But I will keep you yet another night, in payment for which you must tomorrow chop me a load of wood, and make it small."

The soldier spent the whole day in doing it, and in the evening the Witch proposed that he should stay one night more. "Tomorrow, you shall do me a very trifling piece of work. Behind my house, there is an old, dry well, into which my light has fallen. It burns blue, and never goes out, and you shall bring it up again for me."

Next day, the Old Woman took him to the well, and let him down in a basket. He found the Blue Light, and made her a signal to draw him up again. She did draw him up, but when he came near the edge, she stretched down her hand and wanted to take the Blue Light away from him.

"No," said he, perceiving her evil intention, "I will not give you the light, until I am standing with both feet upon the ground."

The Witch fell into a passion, let him down again into the well, and went away.

The poor soldier fell without injury on the moist ground, and the Blue Light went on burning. But of what use was that to him? He saw very well that he could not escape death. He sat for a while very sorrowfully, then suddenly he felt in his pocket and found his

pipe, which was still half full of tobacco. "This shall be my last pleasure," thought he, pulled it out, lit it at the Blue Light and began to smoke.

When the smoke had circled about the cavern, suddenly a little Black Man stood before him, and said, "Master, what are your commands?"

"What commands have I to give you?" replied the soldier, quite astonished.

"I must do everything you bid me," said the Little Man.

"Good," said the soldier; "then in the first place help me out of this well."

The Little Man took him by the hand, and led him through an underground passage, but the soldier did not forget to take the Blue Light with him. On the way the Little Man showed him treasures hidden there, and the soldier took as much gold as he could carry.

When he was above, he said to the Little Man, "Now go and bind the old Witch, and carry her before the judge."

In a short time she, with frightful cries, came riding by, as swift as the wind, on a wild tom-cat, nor was it long after that before the Little Man reappeared. "It is all done," said he, "and the Witch is already hanging on the gallows. What further commands has my lord?" inquired the Little Man.

"At this moment, none," answered the soldier; "you may return home. Only be at hand immediately, if I summon you."

"Nothing more is needed than that you should light your pipe at the Blue Light, and I will appear before you at once." Thereupon he vanished from sight.

The soldier returned to the town from which he had come. He went to the best inn, ordered himself handsome clothes, and then bade the landlord furnish him a room as magnificent as possible.

When it was ready and the soldier had taken possession of it, he summoned the Little Black Man and said, "I have served the King faithfully, but he has dismissed me, and left me to hunger, and now I want to punish him."

"What am I to do?" asked the Little Man.

"Late at night, when the King's Daughter is in bed, bring her here in her sleep; she shall do servant's work for me."

The Little Man said, "That is an easy thing for me to do, but a very dangerous thing for you, for if it is discovered, you will fare ill."

When twelve o'clock had struck, the door sprang open, and the Little Man carried in the Princess.

"Aha! are you there?" cried the soldier, "get to your work at once! Fetch the broom and sweep the chamber."

When she had done this, he ordered her to come to his chair. Then he stretched out his feet and said, "Pull off my boots for me," and made her pick them up again, and clean and brighten them.

She, however, did everything he bade her, without opposition, silently and with half-shut eyes. When the first cock crowed, the Little Man carried her back to the royal Palace, and laid her in her bed.

Next morning, when the Princess arose, she went to her father, and told him that she had had a very strange dream. "I was carried through the streets with the rapidity of lightning," said she, "and taken into a soldier's room, and I had to wait upon him like a servant, sweep his room, clean his boots, and do all kinds of menial work. It was only a dream, and yet I am just as tired as if I really had done everything."

"The dream may have been true," said the King. "I will give you a piece of advice. Fill your pocket full of peas, and make a small hole in it, and then if you are carried away again, they will fall out and leave a track in the streets."

But unseen by the King, the Little Man was standing beside him when he said that, and heard all. At night, when the sleeping Princess was again carried through the streets, some peas certainly did fall out of her pocket, but they made no track, for the crafty Little Man had just before scattered peas in every other street. And again the Princess was compelled to do servant's work until cock-crow.

Next morning, the King sent his people out to seek the track, but it was all in vain, for in every street poor children were sitting, picking up peas, and saying, "It must have rained peas, last night."

"We must think of something else," said the King; "keep your shoes on when you go to bed, and before you come back from the place where you are taken, hide one of them there. I will soon find it."

The Little Black Man heard this plot, and at night when the soldier again ordered him to bring the Princess, revealed it to him, and told him that he knew of no way to overcome this stratagem, and that if the shoe were found in the soldier's house it would go badly with him.

"Do what I bid you," replied the soldier. And again this third night, the Princess was obliged to work like a servant, but before she went away, she hid her shoe under the bed.

Next morning, the King had the entire town searched for his daughter's shoe. It was found at the soldier's, and the soldier himself, who at the entreaty of the Little Man, had gone outside the city-gate, was soon brought back, and thrown into prison.

In his flight he had forgotten the most valuable things he had, the Blue Light and the gold, and had only one ducat in his pocket. And now loaded with chains, he was standing at the window of his dungeon, when he chanced to see one of his comrades passing by.

The soldier tapped at the pane of glass, and when this man came up, said to him, "Be so kind as to fetch me the small bundle I have left lying in the inn, and I will give you a ducat for doing it."

His comrade ran thither and brought him what he wanted. As soon as the soldier was alone again, he lighted his pipe and summoned the Little Black Man.

"Have no fear," said the latter to his master. "Go wheresoever they take you, and let them do what they will, only take the Blue Light with you."

Next day the soldier was tried, and though he had done nothing wicked, the judge condemned him to death. When he was led forth to die, he begged a last favor of the King.

"What is it?" asked the King.

"That I may smoke one more pipe on my way."

"You may smoke three," answered the King, "but do not imagine that I will spare your life."

Then the soldier pulled out his pipe and lighted it at the

Blue Light. And as soon as a few wreaths of smoke had ascended the Little Man was there with a small cudgel in his hand, and said, "What does my lord command?"

"Strike down to earth that false judge there, and his constable, and spare not the King who has treated me so ill."

Then the Little Man fell on them like lightning, darting this way and that, and whosoever was so much as touched by his cudgel fell to earth, and did not venture to stir again. The King was terrified; he threw himself on the soldier's mercy, and begged merely to be allowed to live. He gave him his kingdom for his own, and the Princess to wife.

THE SPINDLE,
THE SHUTTLE,
AND THE NEEDLE

There was once a girl whose father and mother died while she was still a little child. All alone, in a small house at the end of the village, dwelt her godmother, who supported herself by spinning, weaving, and sewing. The old woman took the forlorn child to live with her, kept her to her work, and educated her in all that is good.

When the girl was fifteen, the old woman became ill, called the child to her bedside, and said, "Dear Daughter, I feel my end drawing near. I leave you the little house, which will protect you from wind and weather, and my spindle, shuttle, and needle, with which you can earn your bread."

Then she laid her hands on the girl's head, blessed her, and said, "Only preserve the love of God in your heart, and all will go well with you."

Thereupon she closed her eyes, and when she was laid in

the earth, the maiden followed the coffin, weeping bitterly, and paid her the last mark of respect.

And now the maiden lived quite alone in the little house, and was industrious, and span, wove, and sewed, and the blessing of the good old woman was on all that she did. It seemed as if the flax in the room increased of its own accord, and whenever she wove a piece of cloth or carpet, or had made a shirt, she at once found a buyer who paid her amply for it. So that she was in want of nothing, and even had something to share with others.

About this time, the Son of the King was traveling about the country looking for a Bride. He was not to choose a poor one, and did not want to have a rich one. So he said, "She shall be my wife who is the poorest, and at the same time the richest."

When he came to the village where the maiden dwelt, he inquired, as he did wherever he went, who was the richest and also the poorest girl in the place? They first named the richest; the poorest, they said, was the girl who lived in the small house quite at the end of the village.

The rich girl was sitting in all her splendor before the door of her house, and when the Prince approached her, she got up, went to meet him, and made him a low curtsey. He looked at her, said nothing, and rode on.

When he came to the house of the poor girl, she was not standing at the door, but sitting in her little room. He stopped his horse, and saw, through the window on which the bright sun was shining, the girl sitting at her spinning-wheel, busily spinning. She looked up, and when she saw that the Prince was gazing in, blushed all over her face, let her eyes fall, and went on spinning. I do not know whether, just at that moment, the thread was quite even; but she went on spinning until the King's Son had ridden away again.

Then she stepped to the window, opened it, and said, "It is so warm in this room!" but she still looked after him as long as she could see the white feathers in his hat. Then she sat down to work again in her own room and went on with her spinning. And a saying which the old woman had often repeated when she was sitting at her work, came into her mind, and she sang these words to herself:

> "*Spindle, my Spindle, haste, haste thee away,*
> *Here to my house bring the wooer, I pray.*"

And what do you think happened? The spindle sprang out of her hand in an instant, and out of the door. And when, in her astonishment, she got up and looked after it, she saw that it was dancing out merrily into the open country, and drawing a shining golden thread after it. Before long, it had entirely vanished from her sight.

As she had now no spindle, the girl took the weaver's shuttle in her hand, sat down to her loom, and began to weave.

The spindle, however, danced continually onward, and just as the thread came to an end, reached the Prince.

"What do I see?" he cried; "the spindle certainly wants to show me the way!" He turned his horse about, and rode back with the golden thread. The girl was, however, sitting at her work singing:

> "*Shuttle, my Shuttle, weave well this day,*
> *And guide the wooer to me, I pray.*"

Immediately the shuttle sprang out of her hand and out by the door. Before the threshold, however, it began to weave a carpet which was more beautiful than the eyes of man had ever yet beheld. Lilies and roses blossomed on both sides of it. And on a golden ground in the centre green branches ascended, under which bounded hares and rabbits. Stags and deer stretched their heads in between them. Brightly-colored birds were sitting in the branches above. They lacked nothing but the gift of song. The shuttle leapt hither and thither, and everything seemed to grow of its own accord.

As the shuttle had run away, the girl sat down to sew. She held the needle in her hand and sang:

"Needle, my Needle, sharp-pointed and fine,
Prepare for a wooer this house of mine."

Then the needle leapt out of her fingers, and flew everywhere about the room as quick as lightning. It was just as if invisible spirits were working. They covered tables and benches with green cloth in an instant, and the chairs with velvet, and hung the windows with silken curtains.

Hardly had the needle put in the last stitch, than the maiden saw through the window the white feathers of the Prince, whom the spindle had brought thither by the golden thread. He alighted, stepped over the carpet into the house, and when he entered the room, there stood the maiden in her poor garments, but she shone out from them like a rose surrounded by leaves.

"You are the poorest and also the richest," said he to her. "Come with me, you shall be my Bride."

She did not speak, but she gave him her hand. Then he kissed her, and led her forth, lifted her on to his horse, and took her to the royal castle, where the wedding was solemnized with great rejoicings.

The spindle, shuttle, and needle were preserved in the treasure-chamber, and held in great honor.

THE THREE
LUCK-CHILDREN

A father once called his three sons before him. He gave to
the first a cock, to the second a scythe, and to the third a cat.

"I am old," said he, "my death is nigh, and I have wished
to take thought for you before my end. Money I have not, and
what I now give you seems of little worth. But all depends
on your making a sensible use of it. Only seek out a country
where such things are still unknown, and your fortune is
made."

After the father's death, the eldest went away with his
cock. But wherever he came the cock was already known. In
the towns, he saw him from a long distance, sitting upon the
steeples and turning round with the wind; and in the villages
he heard more than one crowing. No one would show any
wonder at the creature, so that it did not look as if he would
make his fortune by it.

At last, however, it happened that he came to an island
where the people knew nothing about cocks, and did not even
understand how to tell time. They certainly knew when it was

morning or evening. But at night, if they did not sleep through it, not one of them knew how to find out the time.

"Look!" said he, "what a proud creature! It has a ruby-red crown upon its head, and wears spurs like a knight. It calls you three times during the night, at fixed hours; and when it calls for the last time, the sun soon after rises. But if it crows by broad daylight, then take notice, for there will certainly be a change of weather."

The people were well pleased. For a whole night they did not sleep, and listened with great delight as the cock at two, four, and six o'clock, loudly and clearly proclaimed the time. They asked if the creature were for sale, and how much he wanted for it.

"About as much gold as an ass can carry," answered he.

"A ridiculously small price for such a precious creature!" they cried all together, and willingly gave him what he had asked.

When he came home with his wealth, his brothers were astonished, and the second said, "Well, I will go forth and see whether I cannot get rid of my scythe as profitably." But it did not look as if he would, for laborers met him everywhere, and they had scythes upon their shoulders as well as he.

At last, however, he chanced upon an island where the people knew nothing of scythes. When the corn was ripe, they took cannon out to the fields and shot it down. Now this was rather an uncertain affair. Many shot right over it, others hit the ears instead of the stems and shot them away, whereby much was lost; and besides all this it made a terrible noise.

So the man set to work and mowed it down so quietly and quickly that the people opened their mouths with astonishment. They agreed to give him what he wanted for the scythe, and he received a horse laden with as much gold as it could carry.

And now the third brother wanted to take his cat to the right man. He fared just like the others. So long as he stayed on the mainland, there was nothing to be done. Every place had cats, and there were so many of them that most new-born kittens were drowned in the ponds.

At last, he sailed to an island, and it luckily happened that no cats had ever yet been seen there, and that the mice had got the upper hand so much, that they danced upon the tables and benches whether the master were at home or not. The people complained bitterly of the plague. The King himself, in his palace, did not know how to secure himself against them. Mice squeaked in every corner, and gnawed whatever they could lay hold of with their teeth.

But now the cat began her chase, and soon cleared a couple of rooms, and the people begged the King to buy the wonderful beast for the country. The King willingly gave what was asked, which was a mule laden with gold; and the third brother came home with the greatest treasure of all.

The cat made merry with the mice in the royal palace, and killed so many that they could not be counted. At last she grew warm with the work and thirsty, so she stood still, lifted up her head and cried, "Mew! mew!"

When they heard this strange cry, the King and all his people were frightened, and in their terror ran out of the palace.

Then the King took counsel what was best to be done. At last, it was decided to send a herald to the cat, and command her to leave the palace; if not, she was to expect that force would be used against her.

The councilors said, "We would rather be plagued with mice to which misfortune we are accustomed, than give up our lives to such a monster as this."

A noble youth, therefore, was sent to ask the cat whether she "would peaceably quit the palace." But the cat, whose thirst had become still greater, answered again, "Mew! Mew!"

The youth thought that she said, "Most certainly not! Most certainly not!" and took this answer to the King.

"Then," said the councilors, "she must yield to force."

Cannon were brought out, and the palace was soon in

flames. When the fire reached the room where the cat was sitting, she sprang safely out of the window. But the besiegers did not leave off, until the whole palace was shot down to the ground.

THE DONKEY CABBAGES

There was once a young huntsman, who went into the forest to lie in wait. He had a fresh and joyous heart, and as he was going thither, whistling upon a leaf, an ugly old crone came up, who spoke to him and said, "Good-day, dear huntsman, truly you are merry and contented, but I am suffering from hunger and thirst, do give me an alms."

The huntsman had compassion on the poor old creature, felt in his pocket, and gave her what he could afford.

He was then about to go further, but the old woman stopped him and said, "Listen, dear Huntsman, to what I tell you. I will make you a present in return for your kindness. Go on your way now, but in a little while you will come to a tree, whereon nine birds are sitting which have a cloak in their claws, and are plucking at it. Take your gun and shoot into the midst of them. They will let the cloak fall down to you, but one of the birds will be hurt, and will drop dead.

"Carry away the cloak, it is a Wishing-Cloak. When you throw it over your shoulders, you only have to wish to be in a certain place, and you will be there in the twinkling of an eye. Take out the heart of the dead bird, swallow it whole, and every morning early, when you get up, you will find a gold piece under your pillow."

The huntsman thanked the Wise Woman, and thought to himself, "Those are fine things that she has promised me, if all does but come true!"

And verily when he had walked about a hundred paces, he heard in the branches above him a screaming and twittering. He looked up and saw a crowd of birds, who were tearing a piece of cloth with their beaks and claws, and tugging and fighting as if each wanted to have it all to himself.

"Well," said the huntsman, "this is wonderful. It has come to pass just as the old wife foretold!" and he took the gun from his shoulder, aimed and fired right into the midst of them, so that the feathers flew about.

The birds instantly took to flight with loud outcries, but one dropped down dead, and the cloak fell at the same time. Then the huntsman did as the old woman had directed him, cut open the bird, sought the heart, swallowed it down, and took the cloak home with him.

Next morning, when he awoke, the promise occurred to him. He wished to see if it also had been fulfilled. When he lifted up the pillow, the gold piece shone in his eyes. The next day, he found another, and so it went on, every time he got up. He gathered together a heap of gold, but at last he thought, "Of what use is all my gold to me if I stay at home? I will go forth and see the world."

He then took leave of his parents, buckled on his huntsman's pouch and gun, and went out into the world.

It came to pass, that one day he traveled through a dense forest, and when he came to the end of it, in the plain before him was a fine castle. An Old Woman was standing with a wonderfully beautiful maiden, looking out of one of the windows.

The Old Woman, however, was a Witch and said to the maiden, "There comes a man out of the forest, who has a wonderful treasure in his body. We must filch it from him, my dear Daughter. It is more suitable for us than for him. He has a bird's heart about him, by means of which every morning, a gold piece lies under his pillow." She told her what she was to do to get it, and what part she had to play, and finally threatened her, and said with angry eyes, "And if you do not attend to what I say, it will be the worse for you."

Now when the huntsman came nearer he descried the maiden, and said to himself, "I have traveled about for such a long time, I will take a rest for once, and enter that beautiful castle. I have certainly money enough." Nevertheless, the real reason was that he had caught sight of the pretty maiden.

He entered the house, and was well received and courteously entertained. Before long, he was so much in love with the young Witch that he no longer thought of anything else, and saw things as she saw them, and did what she desired.

The Old Woman then said, "Now we must have the bird's heart, he will never miss it." She prepared a drink, and when it was ready, poured it into a cup and gave it to the maiden, who was to present it to the huntsman.

She did so, saying, "Now, my Dearest, drink to me."

So he took the cup, and when he had swallowed the draught, he brought up the heart of the bird. The girl had to take it away secretly and swallow it herself, for the Old Woman would have it so. Thenceforward he found no more gold under his pillow. But it lay instead under that of the maiden, from whence the Old Woman fetched it away every morning. But he was so much in love and so befooled, that he thought of nothing else but of passing his time with the maiden.

Then the old Witch said, "We have the bird's heart, but we must also take the Wishing-Cloak away from him."

The maiden answered, "We will leave him that; he has lost his wealth."

The Old Woman was angry and said, "Such a mantle is a wonderful thing, and is seldom to be found in this world. I must and will have it!" She gave the maiden several blows, and said that if she did not obey, it should fare ill with her.

So she did the Old Woman's bidding, placed herself at the window and looked on the distant country, as if she were very sorrowful.

The huntsman asked, "Why do you stand there so sorrowfully?"

"Ah, my Beloved," was her answer, "over yonder lies the Garnet Mountain, where the precious stones grow. I long for them so much that when I think of them, I feel quite sad, but who can get them? Only the birds; they fly and can reach them, but a man never."

"Have you nothing else to complain of?" said the huntsman. "I will soon remove that burden from your heart."

With that he drew her under his mantle, wished himself on the Garnet Mountain. In the twinkling of an eye they were sitting on it together. Precious stones were glistening on every side, so that it was a joy to see them. Together they gathered the finest and costliest of them.

Now, the Old Woman had, through her sorceries, contrived that the eyes of the huntsman should become heavy. He said to the maiden, "We will sit down and rest a while. I am so tired, that I can no longer stand on my feet."

Then they sat down, and he laid his head in her lap, and fell asleep. When he was asleep, she unfastened the mantle from his shoulders, and wrapped herself in it, picked up the garnets and stones, and wished herself back at home with them.

But when the huntsman had had his sleep out, he awoke, and perceived that his sweetheart had betrayed him, and left him alone on the wild mountain. Then he said, "Oh, what treachery there is in the world!" and sat there in care and sorrow, not knowing what to do.

But the mountain belonged to some wild and monstrous Giants, who dwelt thereon and lived their lives there, and he had not sat long, before he saw three of them coming toward him. The Giants came up, and the first kicked him with his foot and said, "What sort of an earthworm is lying curled up here?"

The second said, "Step upon him and kill him."

But the third said, "Would that be worth your while? Let him live, he cannot remain here. When he climbs higher, toward the summit of the mountain, the clouds will lay hold of him and bear him away." So saying they passed by.

But the Huntsman had paid heed to their words, and as soon as they were gone, he rose and climbed up to the summit of the mountain. And when he had sat there a while, a cloud floated toward him, caught him up, carried him away, and traveled about for a long time in the heavens. Then it sank lower, and let itself down on a great cabbage-garden, girt round by walls, so that he came softly to the ground on cabbages and vegetables.

Then the huntsman looked about him, and said, "If I only had something to eat! I am so hungry, and my hunger will grow greater. But I see here neither apples nor pears, nor any other sort of fruit, everywhere there is nothing but cabbages." At length he thought, "At a pinch I can eat some of the leaves. They do not taste particularly good, but they will refresh me."

With that he picked himself out a fine head of cabbage, and ate it. But scarcely had he swallowed a couple of mouthfuls, when wonderful! he felt quite changed.

Four legs grew on him, a large head and two thick ears; and he saw with horror that he was changed into a Donkey. Still as his hunger became greater every minute, and as the juicy leaves were suitable to his present nature, he went on eating with great zest. At last he arrived at a different kind of cabbage, but as soon as he had swallowed it, he again felt a change, and resumed his human shape.

Then the huntsman lay down, and slept off his fatigue. When he awoke next morning, he broke off one head of the bad cabbages and another of the good ones, and thought to himself, "This shall help me to get my own again and punish treachery."

Then he took the cabbages with him, climbed over the wall, and went forth to seek for the castle of his sweetheart.

After wandering about for a couple of days, he was lucky enough to find it again. He dyed his face brown, so that his own mother would not have known him; and begged for shelter. "I am so tired," said he, "that I can go no further."

The Witch asked, "Who are you, Countryman, and what is your business?"

Said he, "I have been so fortunate as to find the most wonderful salad which grows under the sun, and am carrying it about with me."

When the Old Woman heard of the exquisite salad, she was greedy, and said, "Dear Countryman, let me just taste this wonderful salad."

"Why not?" answered he, "I have brought two heads with me, and will give you one of them," and he opened his pouch and handed her the bad cabbage.

The Witch suspected nothing amiss, and her mouth watered so for this new dish, that she herself went into the kitchen and prepared it. When it was ready she could not wait until it was set on the table, but took a couple of leaves at once, and put them in her mouth. Hardly had she swallowed them, than she was deprived of her human shape, and she ran out into the courtyard in the form of a Donkey.

Presently the maid-servant entered the kitchen, saw the salad standing there ready prepared, and was about to carry it up. But on the way, according to habit, she was seized by the desire to taste, and she ate a couple of leaves. Instantly the magic power showed itself, and she likewise became a Donkey, and ran out to the Old Woman. And the dish of salad fell to the ground.

Meantime the huntsman sat beside the beautiful maiden, and as no one came with the salad and she also was longing for it, she said, "I don't know what has become of the salad."

The huntsman thought, "The salad must have already taken

effect," and said, "I will go to the kitchen and inquire about it."

As he went down he saw the two Donkeys running about in the courtyard.The salad, however, was lying on the ground. "All right," said he, "the two have taken their portion," and he picked up the other leaves, laid them on the dish, and carried them to the maiden. "I bring you the delicate food myself," said he, "in order that you may not have to wait longer."

Then she ate of it, and was, like the others, immediately deprived of her human form, and ran out into the courtyard in the shape of a Donkey.

After the huntsman had washed his face, so that the transformed ones could recognize him, he went down into the courtyard, and said, "Now you shall receive the wages of your treachery," and bound them together, all three with one rope, and drove them along until he came to a mill.

He knocked at the window, the miller put out his head, and asked what he wanted. "I have three unmanageable beasts," answered he, "which I don't want to keep any longer. Will you take them in, and give them food and stable room, and manage them as I tell you? Then I will pay you what you ask."

The miller said, "Why not? But how am I to manage them?"

The huntsman then said that he was to give three beatings and one meal daily to the old Donkey, and that was the Witch; one beating and three meals to the younger one, which was the servant-girl; and to the youngest, which was the maiden, no beatings and three meals, for he could not bring himself to have the maiden beaten. After that he went back into the castle, and found therein everything he needed.

After a couple of days, the miller came and said he must inform him that the old Donkey which had received three beatings and only one meal daily, was dead; "the two others," he continued, "are certainly not dead, and are fed three times daily, but they are so sad that they cannot last much longer."

The huntsman was moved to pity, put away his anger, and

told the miller to drive them back again to him. And when they came, he gave them some of the good salad, so that they became human again.

The beautiful maiden fell on her knees before him, and said, "Ah, my Beloved, forgive me for the evil I have done you. My mother drove me to it. It was done against my will, for I love you dearly. Your Wishing-Cloak hangs in a cupboard, and as for the Bird's-Heart I will take a potion and bring it up again."

But he thought otherwise, and said, "Keep it. It is all the same, for I will take you for my true wife."

So the wedding was celebrated, and they lived happily together until their death.

CLEVER HANS

The mother of Hans said, "Whither away, Hans?"

Hans answered, "To Grethel."

"Behave well, Hans."

"Oh, I'll behave well. Good-bye, Mother."

"Good-bye, Hans."

Hans comes to Grethel. "Good day, Grethel."

"Good day, Hans. What do you bring that is good?"

"I bring nothing, I want to have something given me."

Grethel presents Hans with a needle.

Hans says, "Good-bye, Grethel."

"Good-bye, Hans."

Hans takes the needle, sticks it into a hay-cart, and follows the cart home. "Good evening, Mother."

"Good evening, Hans. Where have you been?"

"With Grethel."

"What did you take her?"

"Took nothing; had something given me."

"What did Grethel give you?"

"Gave me a needle."

"Where is the needle, Hans?"

"Stuck in the hay-cart."

"That was ill done, Hans. You should have stuck the needle in your sleeve."

"Never mind, I'll do better next time."

"Whither away, Hans?"

"To Grethel, Mother."

"Behave well, Hans."

"Oh, I'll behave well. Good-bye, Mother."

"Good-bye, Hans."

Hans comes to Grethel. "Good day, Grethel."

"Good day, Hans. What do you bring that is good?"

"I bring nothing, I want to have something given me."

Grethel presents Hans with a knife.

"Good-bye, Grethel."

"Good-bye, Hans."

Hans takes the knife, sticks it in his sleeve, and goes home.

"Good evening, Mother."

"Good evening, Hans. Where have you been?"

"With Grethel."

"What did you take her?"

"Took her nothing, she gave me something."

"What did Grethel give you?"

"Gave me a knife."

"Where is the knife, Hans?"

"Stuck it in my sleeve."

"That's ill done, Hans, you should have put the knife in your pocket."

"Never mind, will do better next time."

"Whither away, Hans?"

"To Grethel, Mother."

"Behave well, Hans."

"Oh, I'll behave well. Good-bye, Mother."

"Good-bye, Hans."

Hans comes to Grethel. "Good day, Grethel."

"Good day, Hans. What good thing do you bring?"

"I bring nothing. I want something given me."

Grethel presents Hans with a young goat.

"Good-bye, Grethel."

"Good-bye, Hans."

Hans takes the goat, ties its legs, and puts it in his pocket. When he gets home it is suffocated.

"Good evening, Mother."

"Good evening, Hans. Where have you been?"

"With Grethel."

"What did you take her?"

"Took nothing, she gave me something."

"What did Grethel give you?"

"She gave me a goat."

"Where is the goat, Hans?"

"Put it in my pocket."

"That was ill done, Hans, you should have put a rope round the goat's neck."

"Never mind, will do better next time."

"Whither away, Hans?"

"To Grethel, Mother."

"Behave well, Hans."

"Oh, I'll behave well. Good-bye, Mother."

"Good-bye, Hans."

Hans comes to Grethel. "Good day, Grethel."

"Good day, Hans. What good thing do you bring?"

"I bring nothing, I want something given me."

Grethel presents Hans with a piece of bacon.

"Good-bye, Grethel."

"Good-bye, Hans."

Hans takes the bacon, ties it to a rope, and drags it away behind him. The dogs come and devour the bacon. When he gets home, he has the rope in his hand, and there is no longer anything hanging to it.

"Good evening, Mother."

"Good evening, Hans. Where have you been?"

"With Grethel."

"What did you take her?"

"I took her nothing, she gave me something."

"What did Grethel give you?"

"Gave me a bit of bacon."

"Where is the bacon, Hans?"

"I tied it to a rope, brought it home, dogs took it."

"That was ill done, Hans, you should have carried the bacon on your head."

"Never mind, will do better next time."

"Whither away, Hans?"

"To Grethel, Mother."

"Behave well, Hans."

"I'll behave well. Good-bye, Mother."

"Good-bye, Hans."

Hans comes to Grethel. "Good day, Grethel."

"Good day, Hans. What good thing do you bring?"

"I bring nothing, but would have something given me."

Grethel presents Hans with a calf.

"Good-bye, Grethel."

"Good-bye, Hans."

Hans takes the calf, puts it on his head, and the calf kicks his face.

"Good evening, Mother."

"Good evening, Hans. Where have you been?"

"With Grethel."

"What did you take her?"

"I took nothing, but had something given me."

"What did Grethel give you?"

"A calf."

"Where have you the calf, Hans?"

"I set it on my head and it kicked my face."

"That was ill done, Hans, you should have led the calf, and put it in the stall."

"Never mind, will do better next time."

"Whither away, Hans?"

"To Grethel, Mother."

"Behave well, Hans."

"I'll behave well. Good-bye, Mother."

"Good-bye, Hans."

Hans comes to Grethel. "Good day, Grethel."

"Good day, Hans. What good thing do you bring?"

"I bring nothing, but would have something given me."

Grethel says to Hans, "I will go with you."

Hans takes Grethel, ties her to a rope, leads her to the rack, and binds her fast. Then Hans goes to his mother.

"Good evening, Mother."

"Good evening, Hans. Where have you been?"

"With Grethel."

"What did you take her?"

"I took her nothing."

"What did Grethel give you?"

"She gave me nothing, she came with me."

"Where have you left Grethel?"

"I led her by the rope, tied her to the rack, and scattered some grass for her."

"That was ill done, Hans, you should have cast friendly eyes on her."

"Never mind, will do better."

Hans went into the stable, cut out all the calves' and sheep's eyes, and threw them in Grethel's face. Then Grethel became angry, tore herself lose and ran away, and became the Bride of Hans.

If you enjoyed *Selected Grimm Fairy Tales*, you may like some of the other stories in the Legend Classics series.

Head to your nearest bookstore or look us up online to add another to your collection.

Follow us on Twitter
@legend_press

Follow us on Instagram
@legendpress